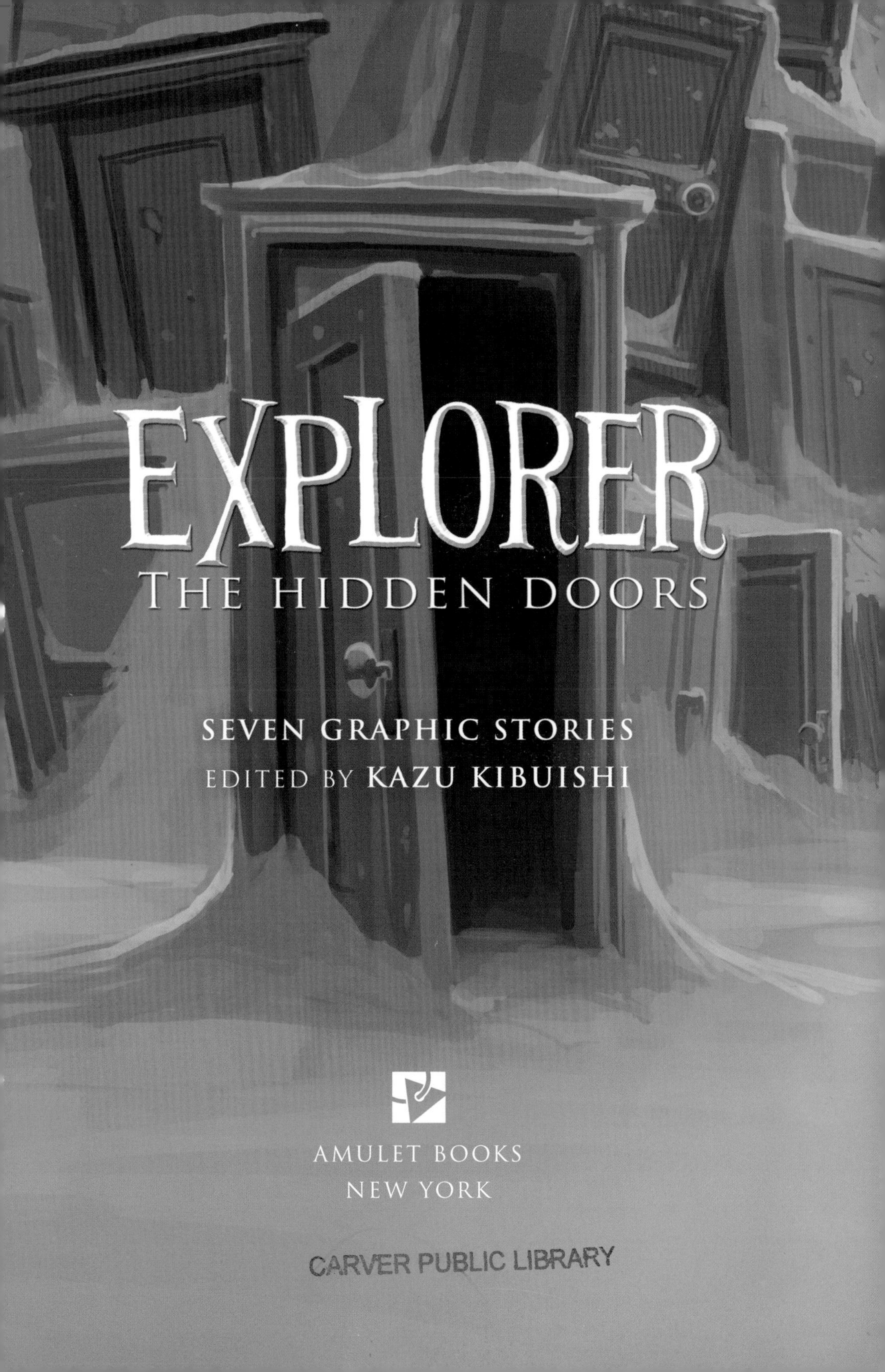

EXPLORER

THE HIDDEN DOORS

SEVEN GRAPHIC STORIES

EDITED BY **KAZU KIBUISHI**

AMULET BOOKS
NEW YORK

THANKS TO MY COEDITORS,
CAROL BURRELL AND JASON CAFFOE
—K.K.

Publisher's Note
This is a work of fiction. Names, characters, places, and incidents are
either the product of the author's imagination or are used fictitiously, and
any resemblance to actual persons, living or dead, business establishments,
events, or locales is entirely coincidental.

Library of Congress Control Number: 2014938941

Paperback ISBN 978-1-4197-0884-8
Hardcover ISBN 978-1-4197-0882-4

Cover art © 2014 Kazu Kibuishi
Compilation © 2014 Bolt City Productions
Book design by Chad W. Beckerman and Jessie Gang

Text and illustrations © 2014 by the individual artists as follows:
"Asteria Crane," pages 4–23, © 2014 Kazu Kibuishi
"The Giant's Kitchen," pages 24–41, © 2014 Jason Caffoe
"Luis 2.0," pages 42–57, © 2014 Jen Wang
"Two-Person Door," pages 58–75, © 2014 Faith Erin Hicks
Fish N Chips in "Spring Cleaning," pages 76–93, © 2014 Steve Hamaker
"Mastaba," pages 94–109, © 2014 Johane Matte
"When Is a Door Not a Door?" pages 110–127, text © 2014 Jen Breach
and Douglas Holgate; illustrations © 2014 Douglas Holgate

Printed and bound in China
10 9 8 7 6 5 4 3 2 1

ABRAMS
THE ART OF BOOKS SINCE 1949
115 West 18th Street
New York, NY 10011
www.abramsbooks.com

CONTENTS

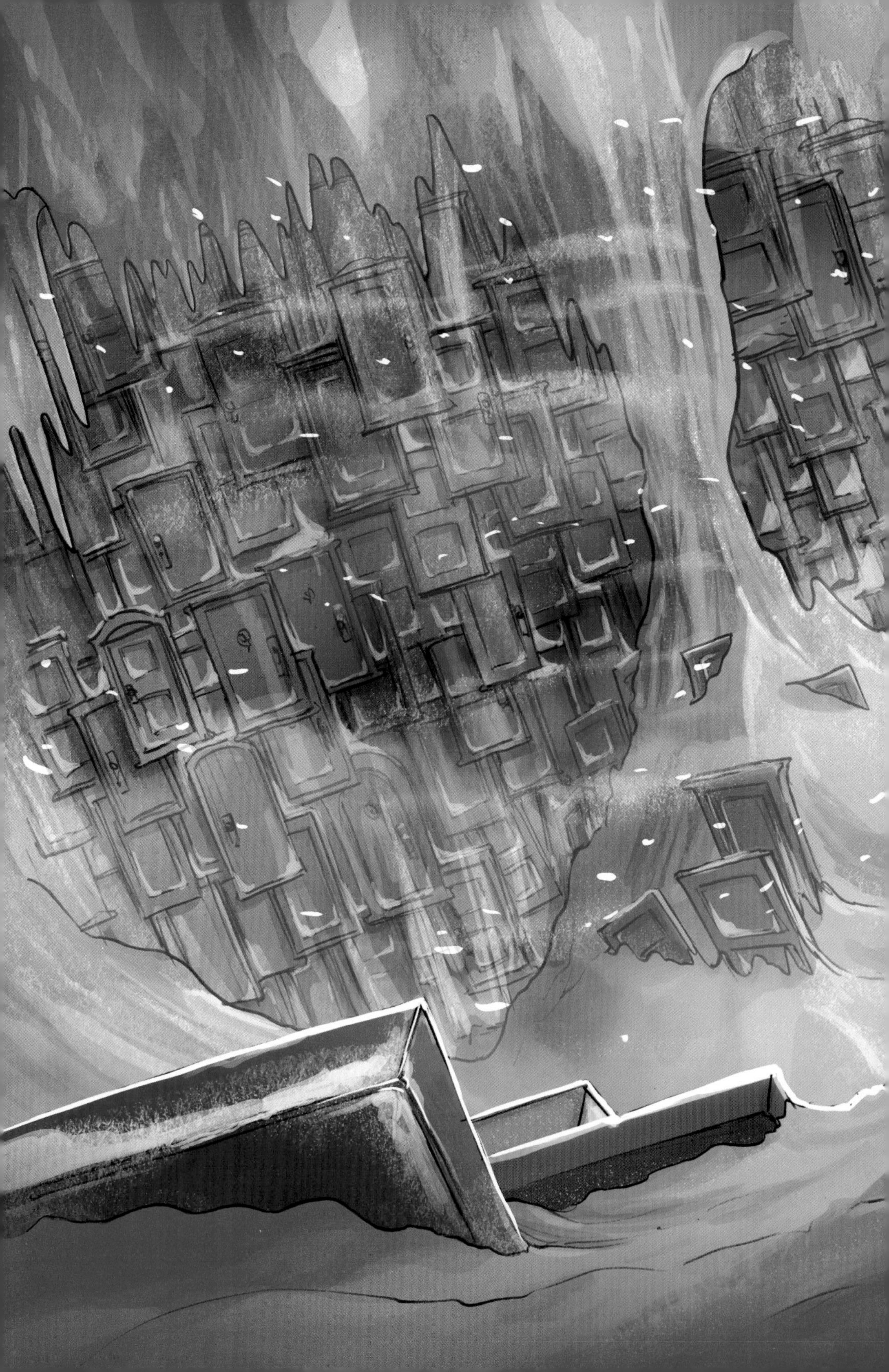

DOCTOR, CAN YOU HEAR ME?
YES, I CAN HEAR YOU, LEN...
ASTERIA CRANE
BY KAZU KIBUISHI
COLORS BY DENVER JACKSON

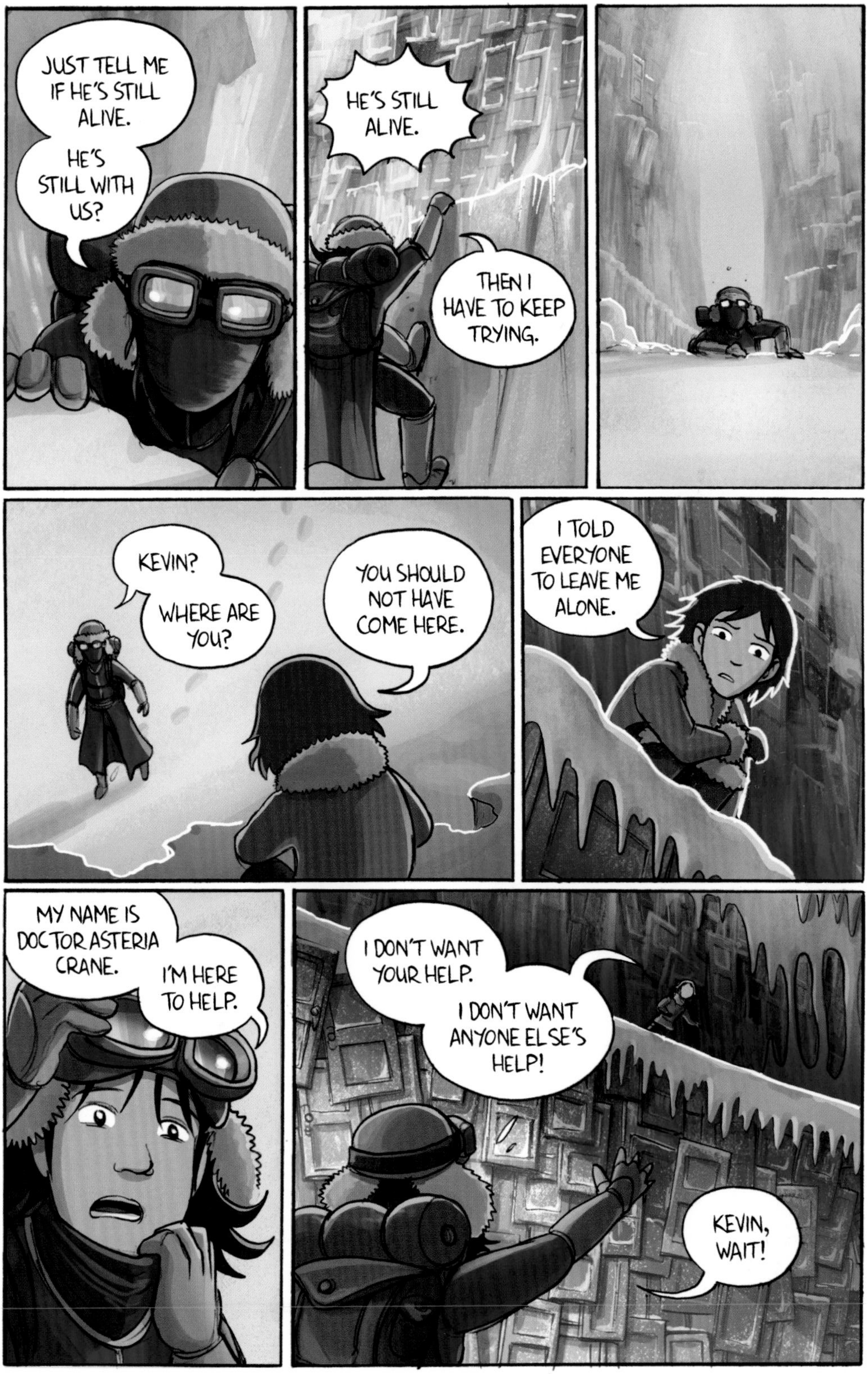
JUST TELL ME IF HE'S STILL ALIVE.
HE'S STILL WITH US?
HE'S STILL ALIVE.
THEN I HAVE TO KEEP TRYING.
KEVIN?
WHERE ARE YOU?
YOU SHOULD NOT HAVE COME HERE.
I TOLD EVERYONE TO LEAVE ME ALONE.
MY NAME IS DOCTOR ASTERIA CRANE.
I'M HERE TO HELP.
I DON'T WANT YOUR HELP.
I DON'T WANT ANYONE ELSE'S HELP!
KEVIN, WAIT!

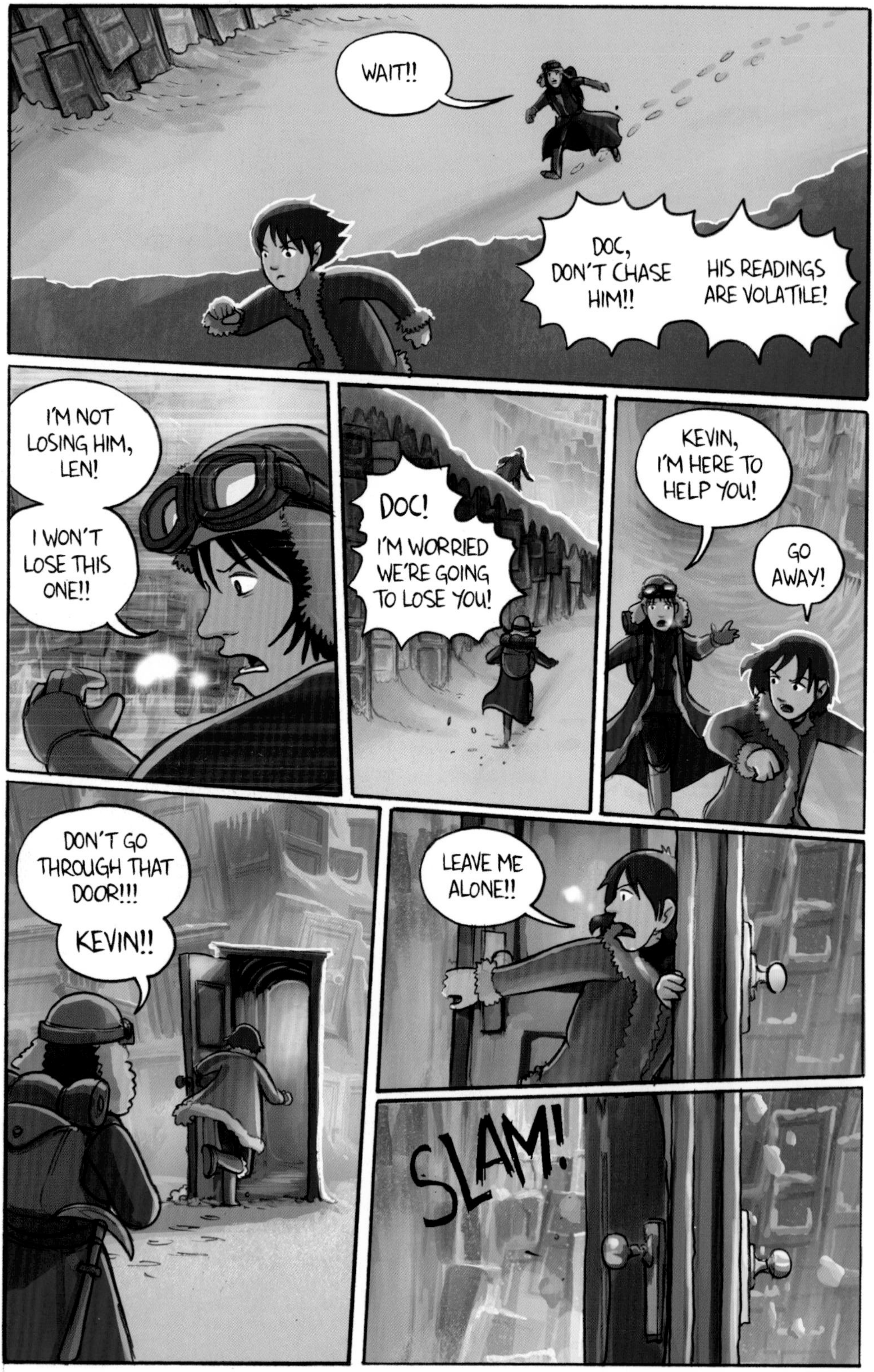
WAIT!!
DOC, DON'T CHASE HIM!!
HIS READINGS ARE VOLATILE!
I'M NOT LOSING HIM, LEN!
I WON'T LOSE THIS ONE!!
DOC!
I'M WORRIED WE'RE GOING TO LOSE YOU!
KEVIN, I'M HERE TO HELP YOU!
GO AWAY!
DON'T GO THROUGH THAT DOOR!!!
KEVIN!!
LEAVE ME ALONE!!
SLAM!

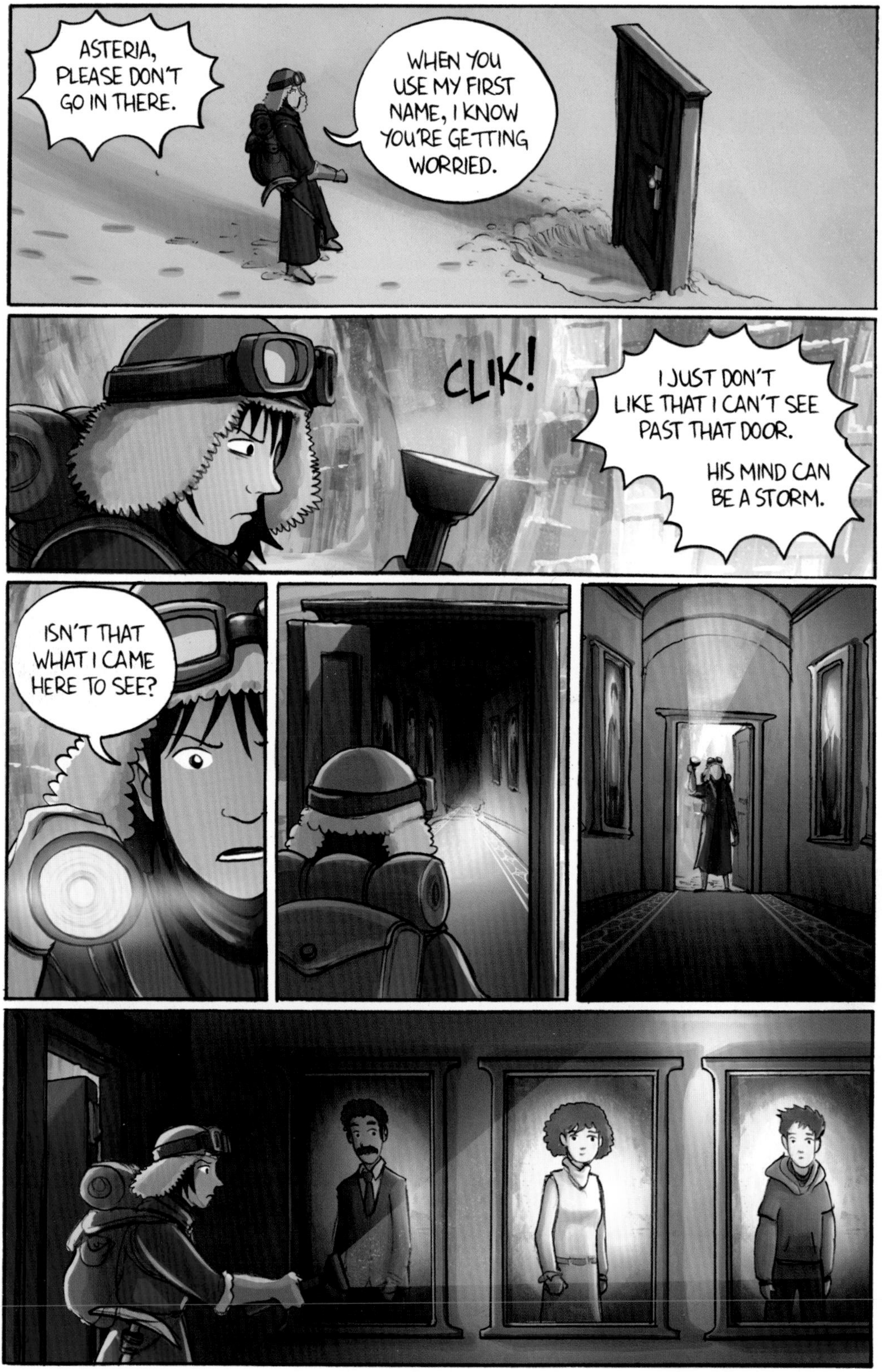
ASTERIA, PLEASE DON'T GO IN THERE.
WHEN YOU USE MY FIRST NAME, I KNOW YOU'RE GETTING WORRIED.
CLIK!
I JUST DON'T LIKE THAT I CAN'T SEE PAST THAT DOOR.
HIS MIND CAN BE A STORM.
ISN'T THAT WHAT I CAME HERE TO SEE?

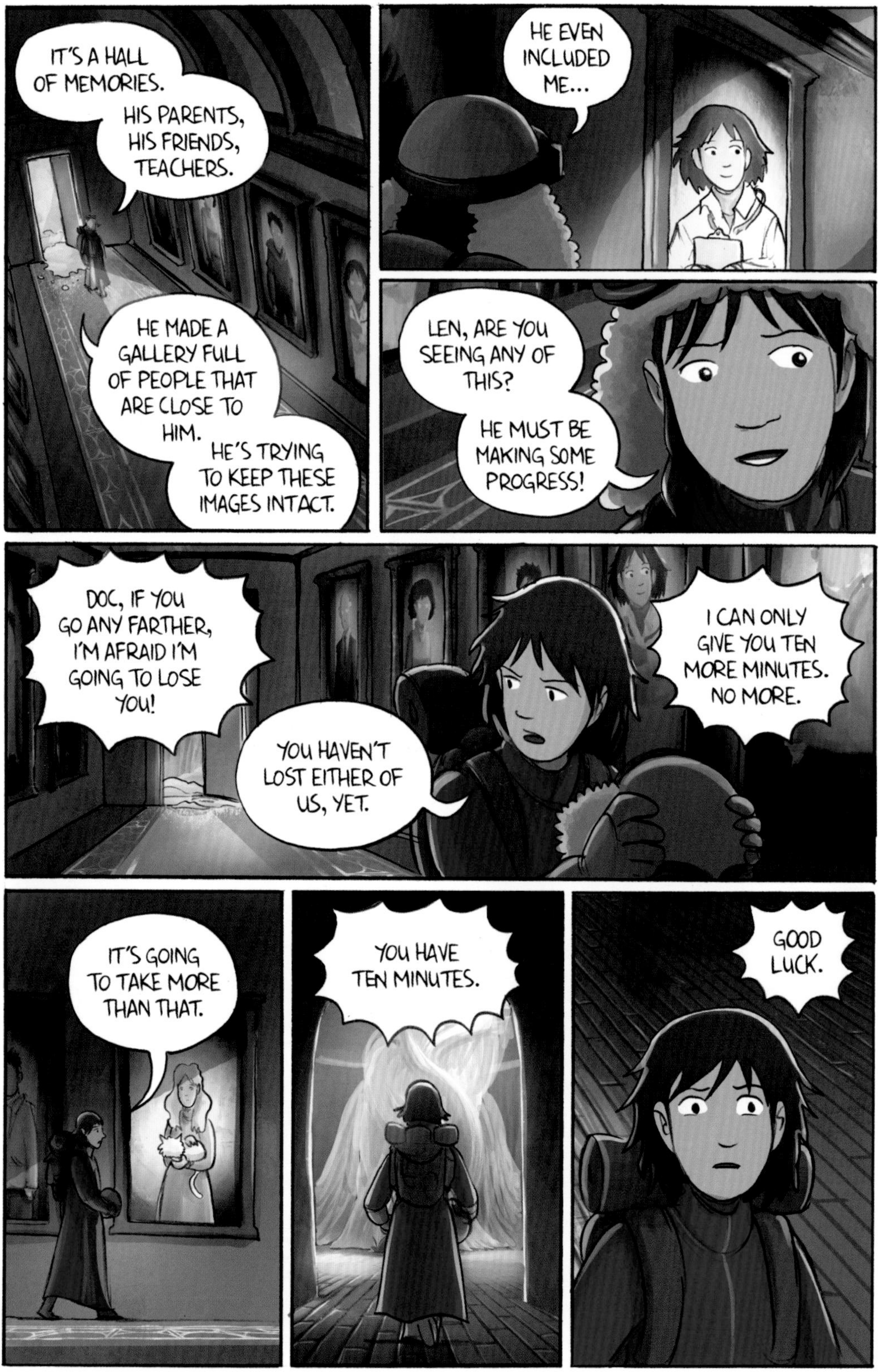
IT'S A HALL OF MEMORIES.
HIS PARENTS, HIS FRIENDS, TEACHERS.
HE MADE A GALLERY FULL OF PEOPLE THAT ARE CLOSE TO HIM.
HE'S TRYING TO KEEP THESE IMAGES INTACT.
HE EVEN INCLUDED ME...
LEN, ARE YOU SEEING ANY OF THIS?
HE MUST BE MAKING SOME PROGRESS!
DOC, IF YOU GO ANY FARTHER, I'M AFRAID I'M GOING TO LOSE YOU!
YOU HAVEN'T LOST EITHER OF US, YET.
I CAN ONLY GIVE YOU TEN MORE MINUTES. NO MORE.
IT'S GOING TO TAKE MORE THAN THAT.
YOU HAVE TEN MINUTES.
GOOD LUCK.

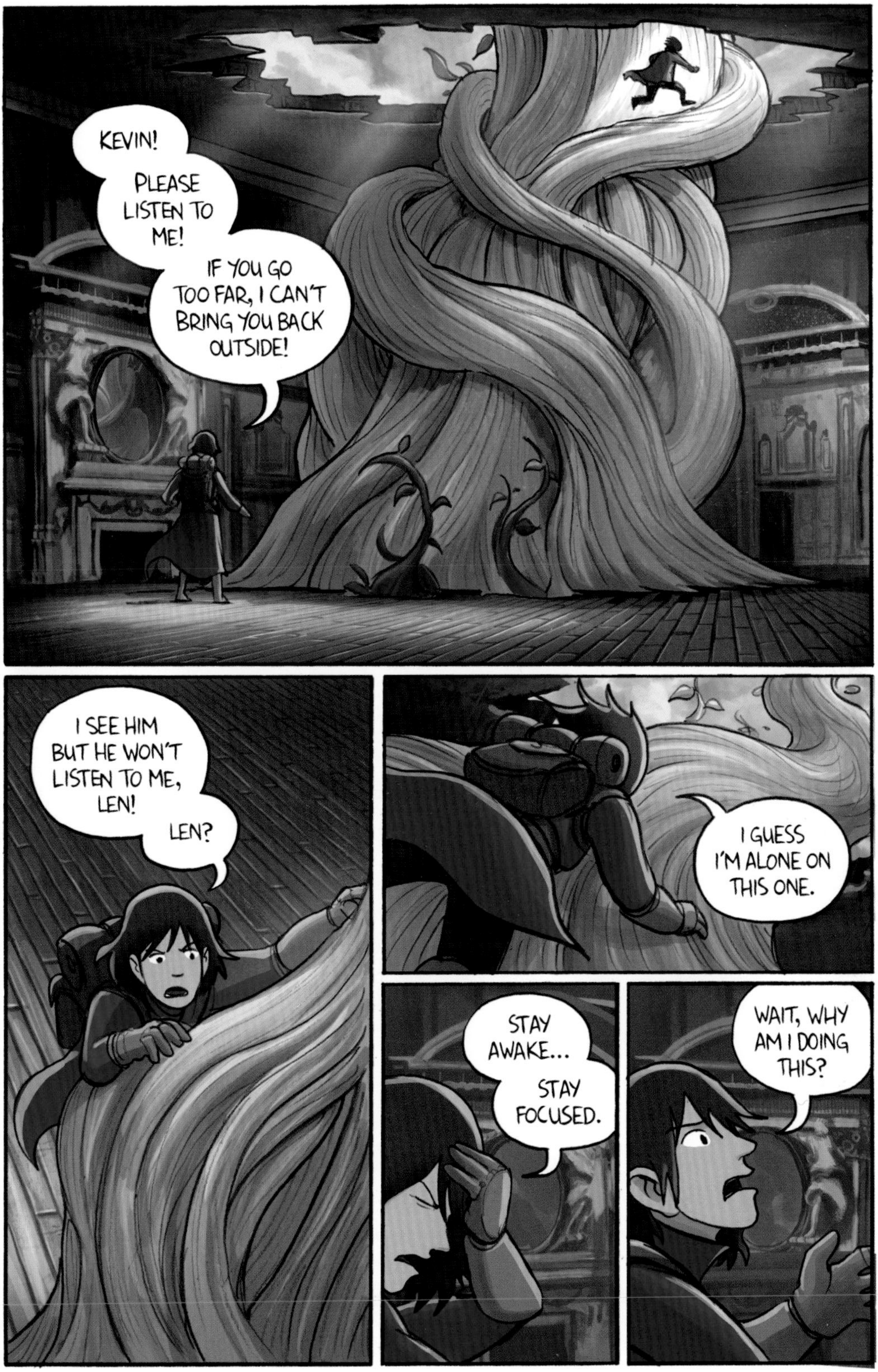
KEVIN!
PLEASE LISTEN TO ME!
IF YOU GO TOO FAR, I CAN'T BRING YOU BACK OUTSIDE!
I SEE HIM BUT HE WON'T LISTEN TO ME, LEN!
LEN?
I GUESS I'M ALONE ON THIS ONE.
STAY AWAKE...
STAY FOCUSED.
WAIT, WHY AM I DOING THIS?

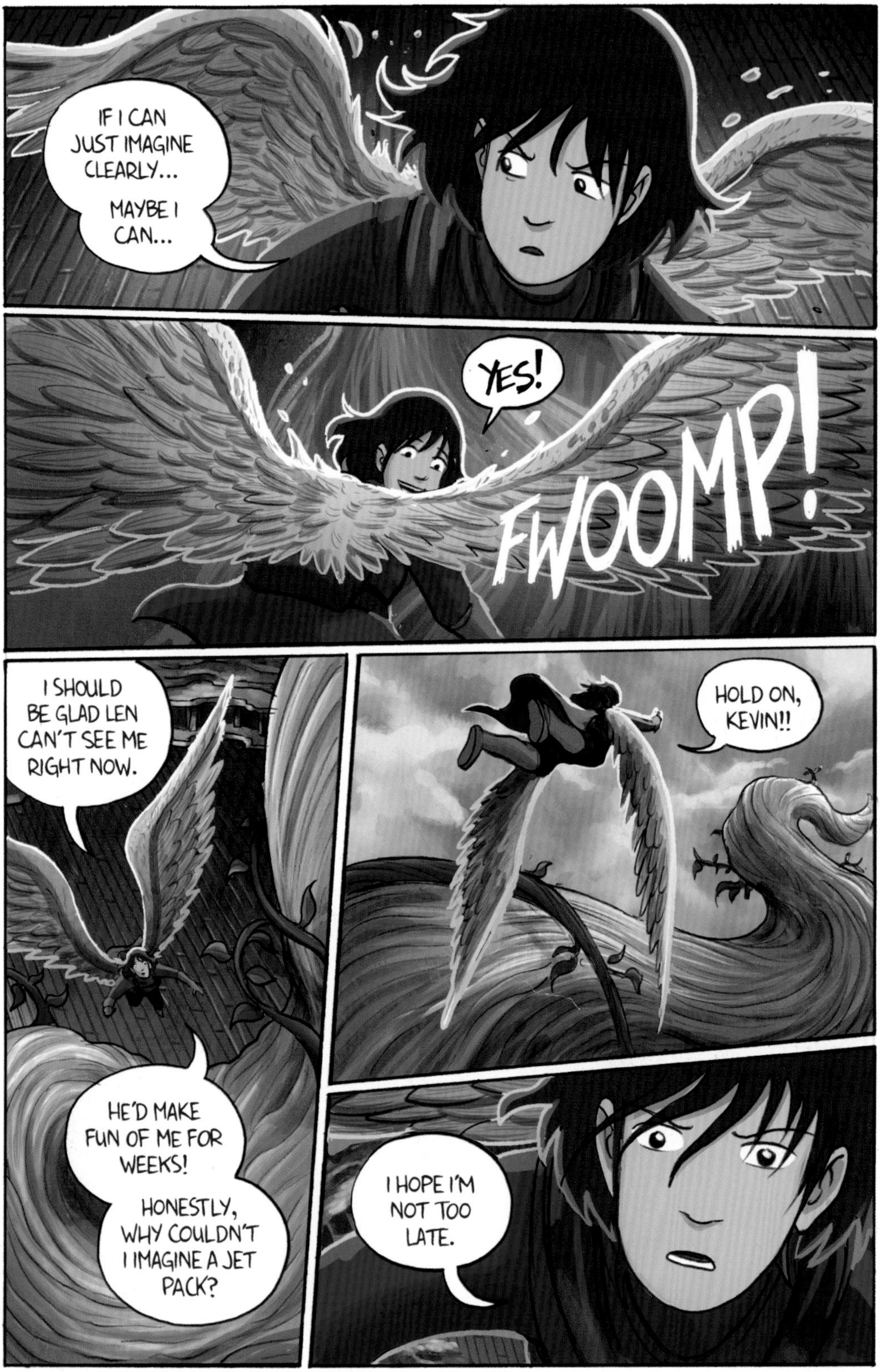
IF I CAN JUST IMAGINE CLEARLY...
MAYBE I CAN...
YES!
FWOOMP!
I SHOULD BE GLAD LEN CAN'T SEE ME RIGHT NOW.
HE'D MAKE FUN OF ME FOR WEEKS!
HONESTLY, WHY COULDN'T I IMAGINE A JET PACK?
HOLD ON, KEVIN!!
I HOPE I'M NOT TOO LATE.

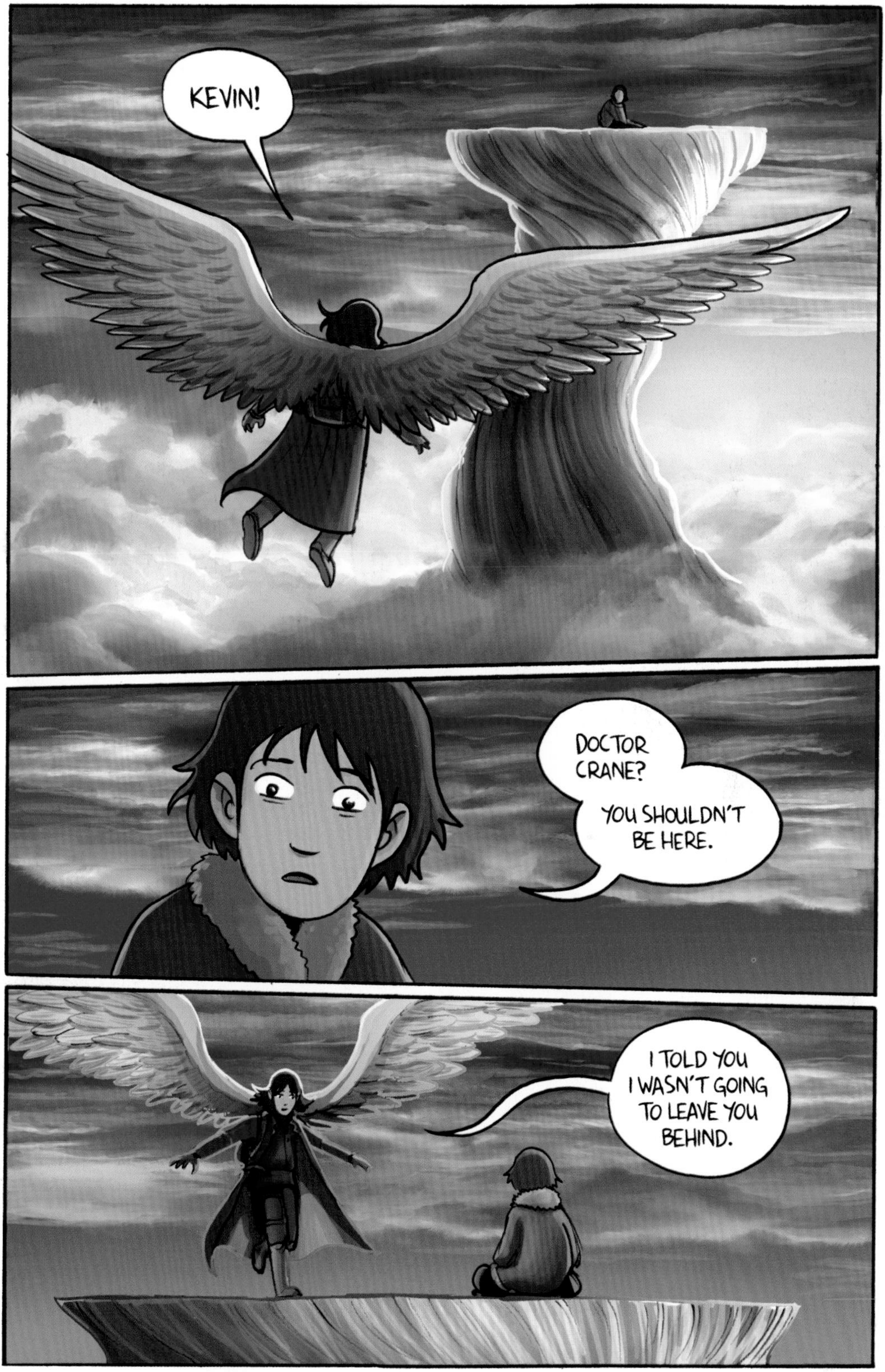
KEVIN!
DOCTOR CRANE?
YOU SHOULDN'T BE HERE.
I TOLD YOU I WASN'T GOING TO LEAVE YOU BEHIND.

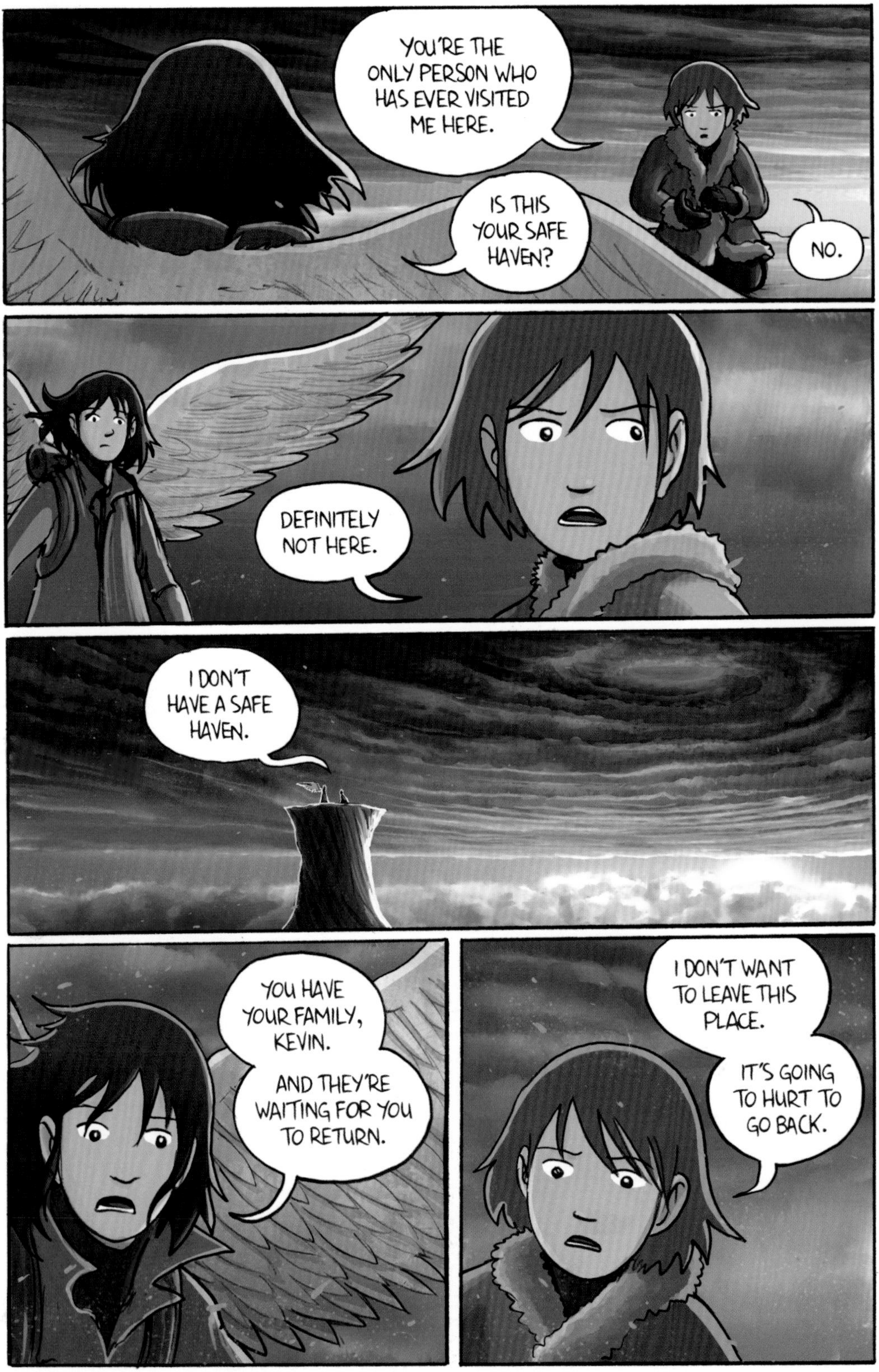
YOU'RE THE ONLY PERSON WHO HAS EVER VISITED ME HERE.
IS THIS YOUR SAFE HAVEN?
NO.
DEFINITELY NOT HERE.
I DON'T HAVE A SAFE HAVEN.
YOU HAVE YOUR FAMILY, KEVIN.
AND THEY'RE WAITING FOR YOU TO RETURN.
I DON'T WANT TO LEAVE THIS PLACE.
IT'S GOING TO HURT TO GO BACK.

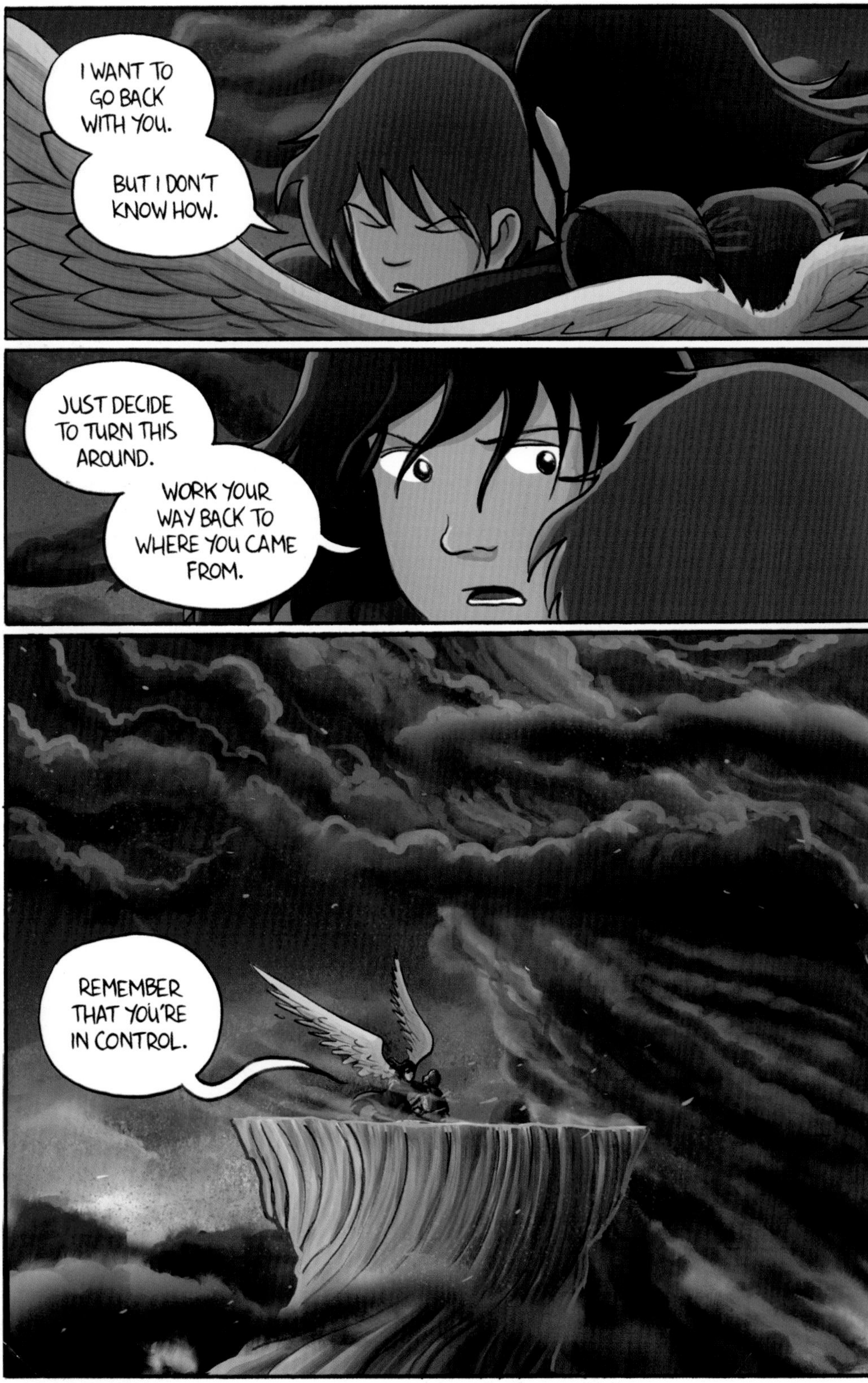
I WANT TO GO BACK WITH YOU.
BUT I DON'T KNOW HOW.
JUST DECIDE TO TURN THIS AROUND.
WORK YOUR WAY BACK TO WHERE YOU CAME FROM.
REMEMBER THAT YOU'RE IN CONTROL.

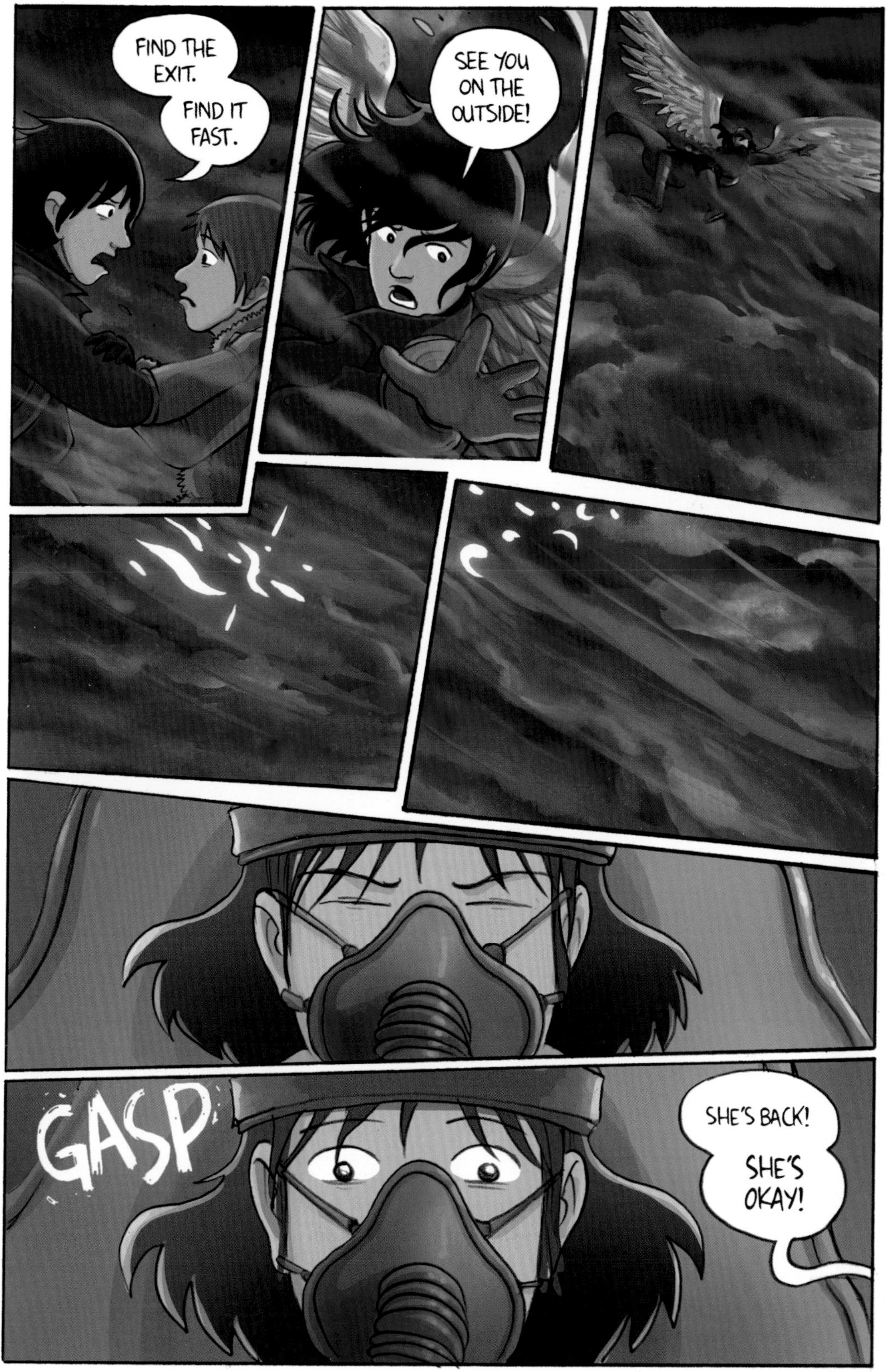
FIND THE EXIT.
FIND IT FAST.
SEE YOU ON THE OUTSIDE!
GASP
SHE'S BACK!
SHE'S OKAY!

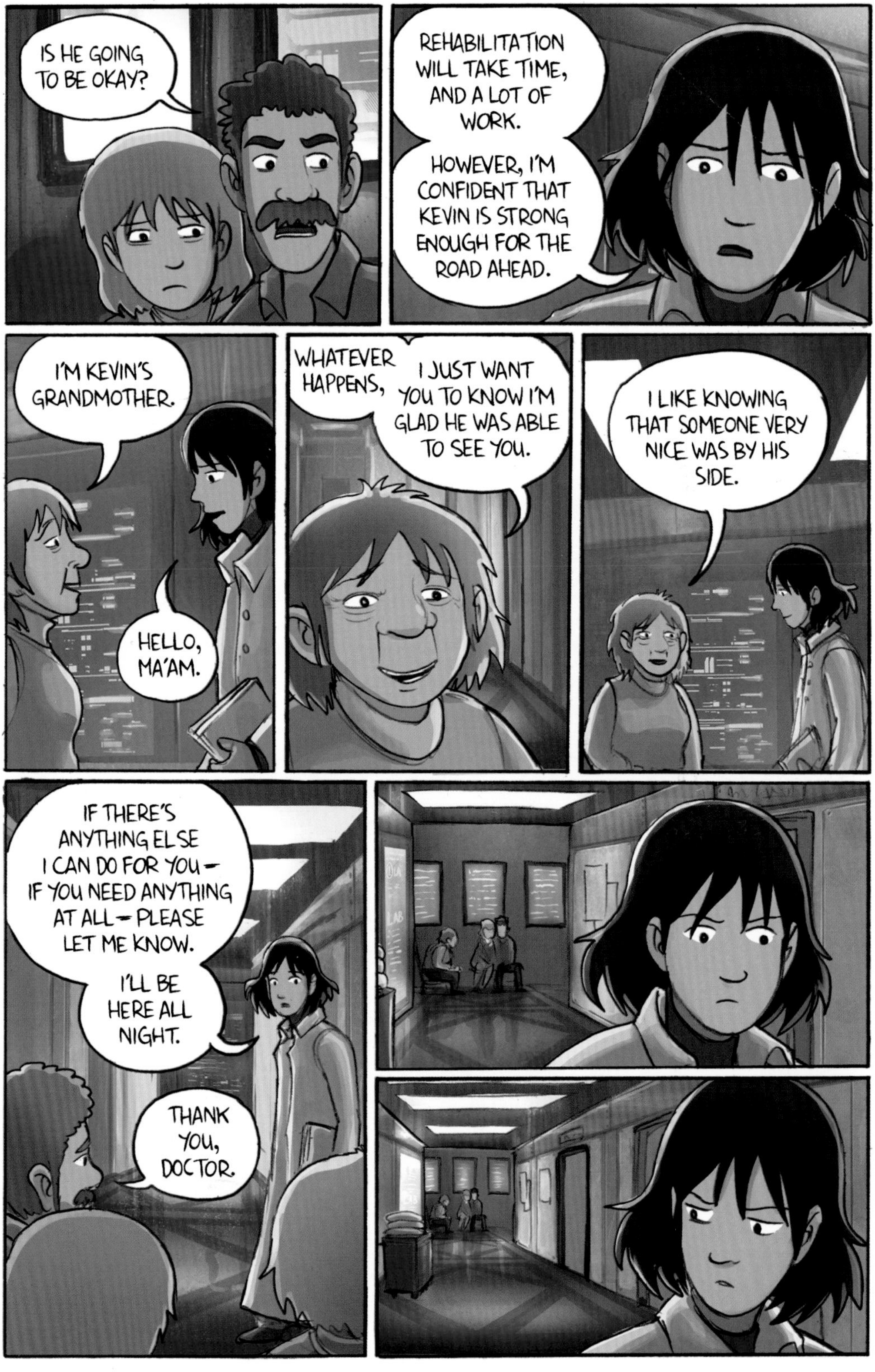
IS HE GOING TO BE OKAY?
REHABILITATION WILL TAKE TIME, AND A LOT OF WORK.
HOWEVER, I'M CONFIDENT THAT KEVIN IS STRONG ENOUGH FOR THE ROAD AHEAD.
I'M KEVIN'S GRANDMOTHER.
HELLO, MA'AM.
WHATEVER HAPPENS,
I JUST WANT YOU TO KNOW I'M GLAD HE WAS ABLE TO SEE YOU.
I LIKE KNOWING THAT SOMEONE VERY NICE WAS BY HIS SIDE.
IF THERE'S ANYTHING ELSE I CAN DO FOR YOU— IF YOU NEED ANYTHING AT ALL—PLEASE LET ME KNOW.
I'LL BE HERE ALL NIGHT.
THANK YOU, DOCTOR.
LAB

CONGRATS, DOC!

IS HE OKAY?

THEY EXPECT A FULL RECOVERY, AND THEY'RE SAYING IT'S THANKS TO YOU.

PHEW.

THANK GOODNESS. ...AND YOU DESERVE JUST AS MUCH CREDIT.

ALL I DID WAS YELL AT YOU THROUGH THE MONITOR.

BUT I WILL TAKE CREDIT FOR GETTING US ANOTHER YEAR OF FUNDING!

LOOKS LIKE WE'LL BE RAIDING PEOPLE'S NIGHTMARES FOR A WHILE.

THE END.

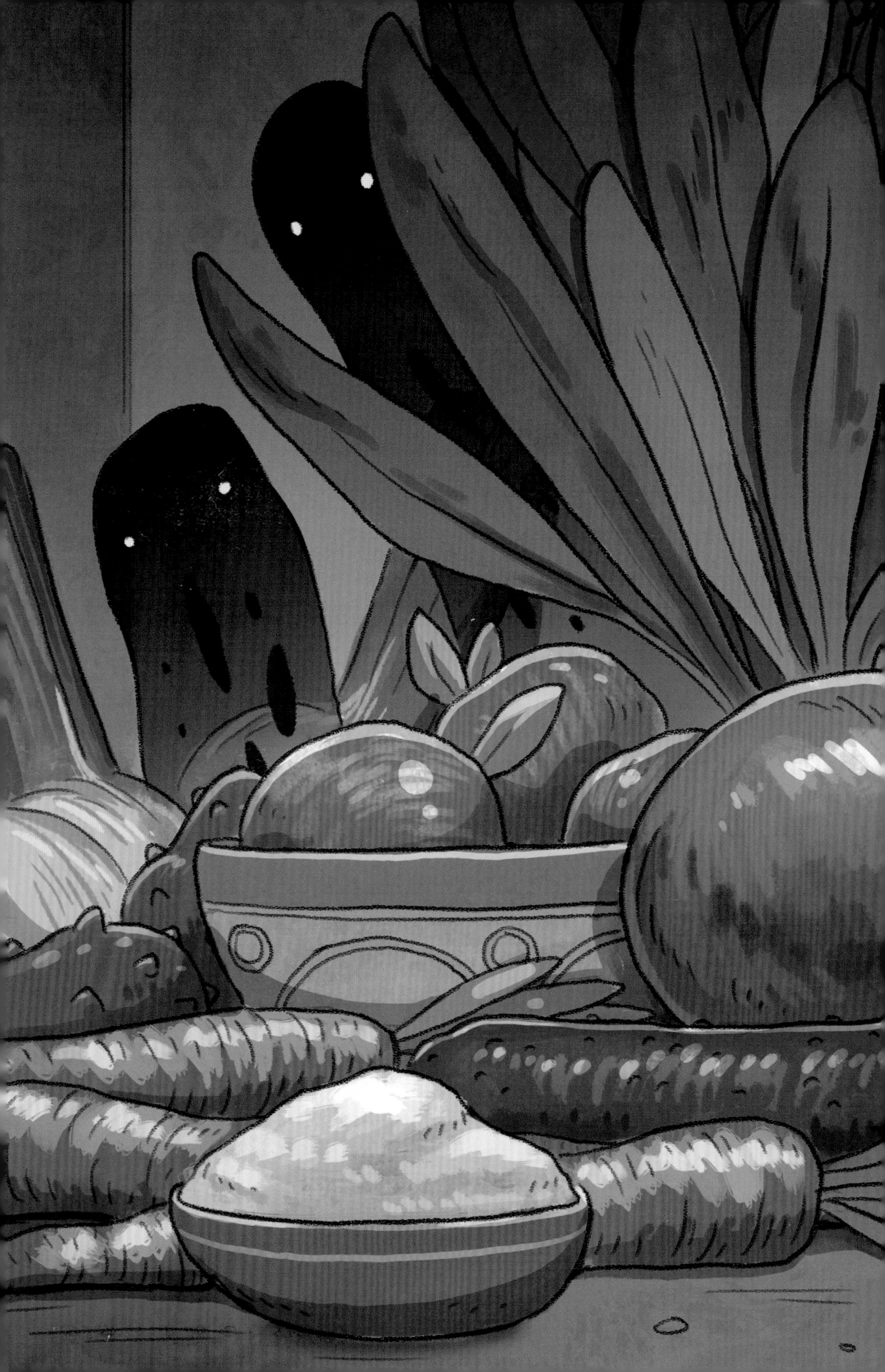

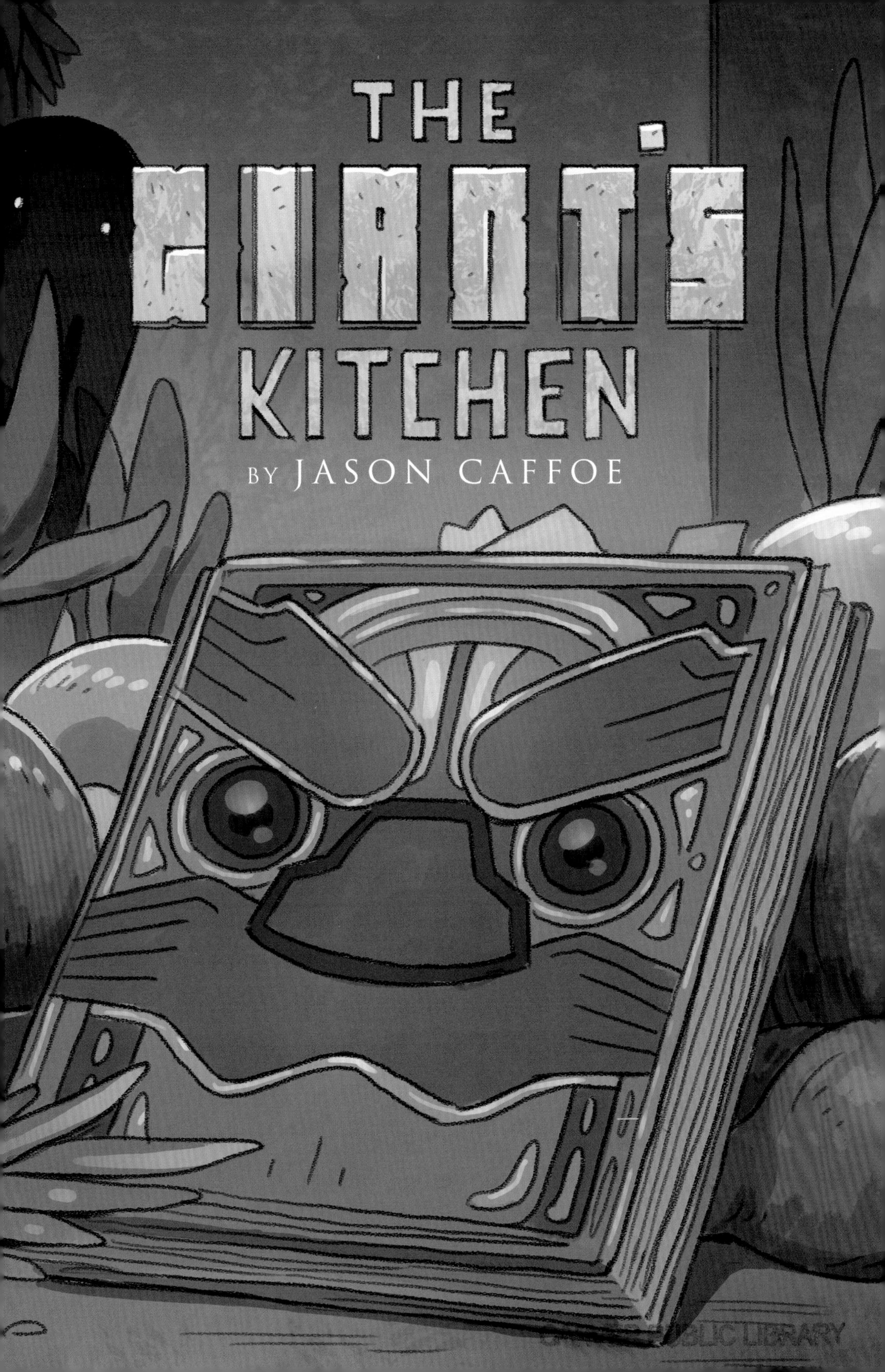
THE GIANT'S KITCHEN
BY JASON CAFFOE

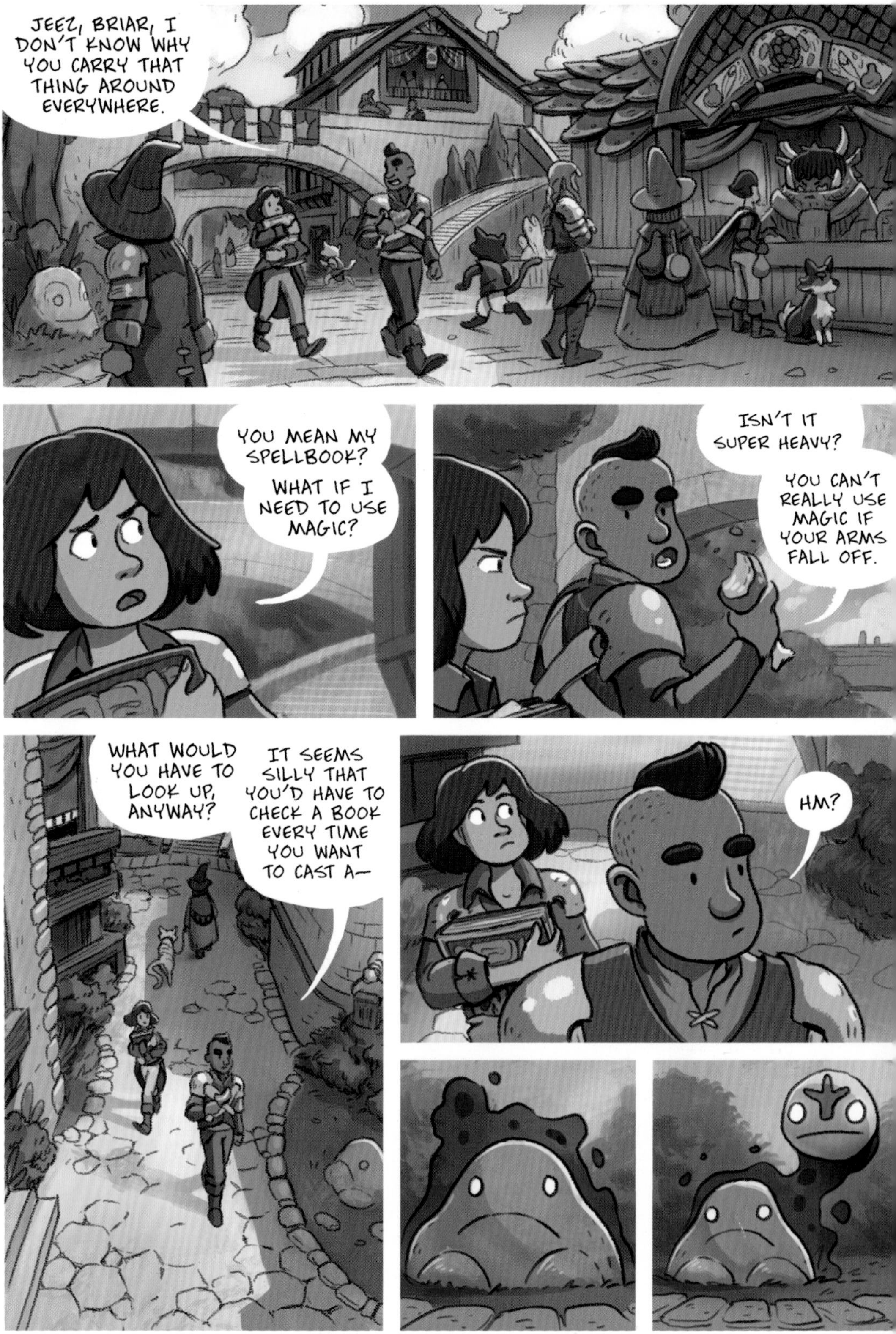
JEEZ, BRIAR, I DON'T KNOW WHY YOU CARRY THAT THING AROUND EVERYWHERE.
YOU MEAN MY SPELLBOOK?
WHAT IF I NEED TO USE MAGIC?
ISN'T IT SUPER HEAVY?
YOU CAN'T REALLY USE MAGIC IF YOUR ARMS FALL OFF.
WHAT WOULD YOU HAVE TO LOOK UP, ANYWAY?
IT SEEMS SILLY THAT YOU'D HAVE TO CHECK A BOOK EVERY TIME YOU WANT TO CAST A—
HM?

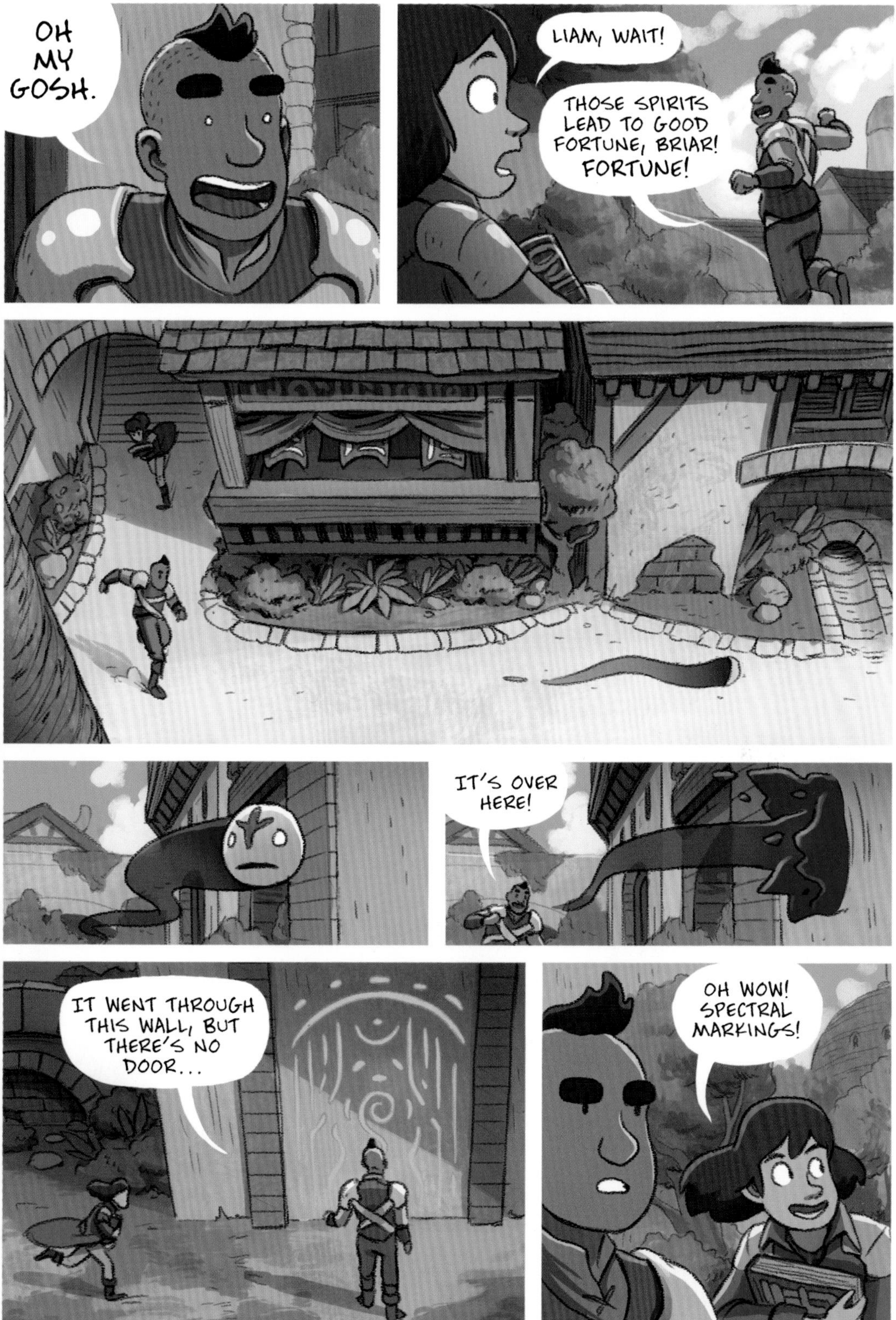
OH MY GOSH.
LIAM, WAIT!
THOSE SPIRITS LEAD TO GOOD FORTUNE, BRIAR! FORTUNE!
IT'S OVER HERE!
IT WENT THROUGH THIS WALL, BUT THERE'S NO DOOR...
OH WOW! SPECTRAL MARKINGS!

KRAKOOOM

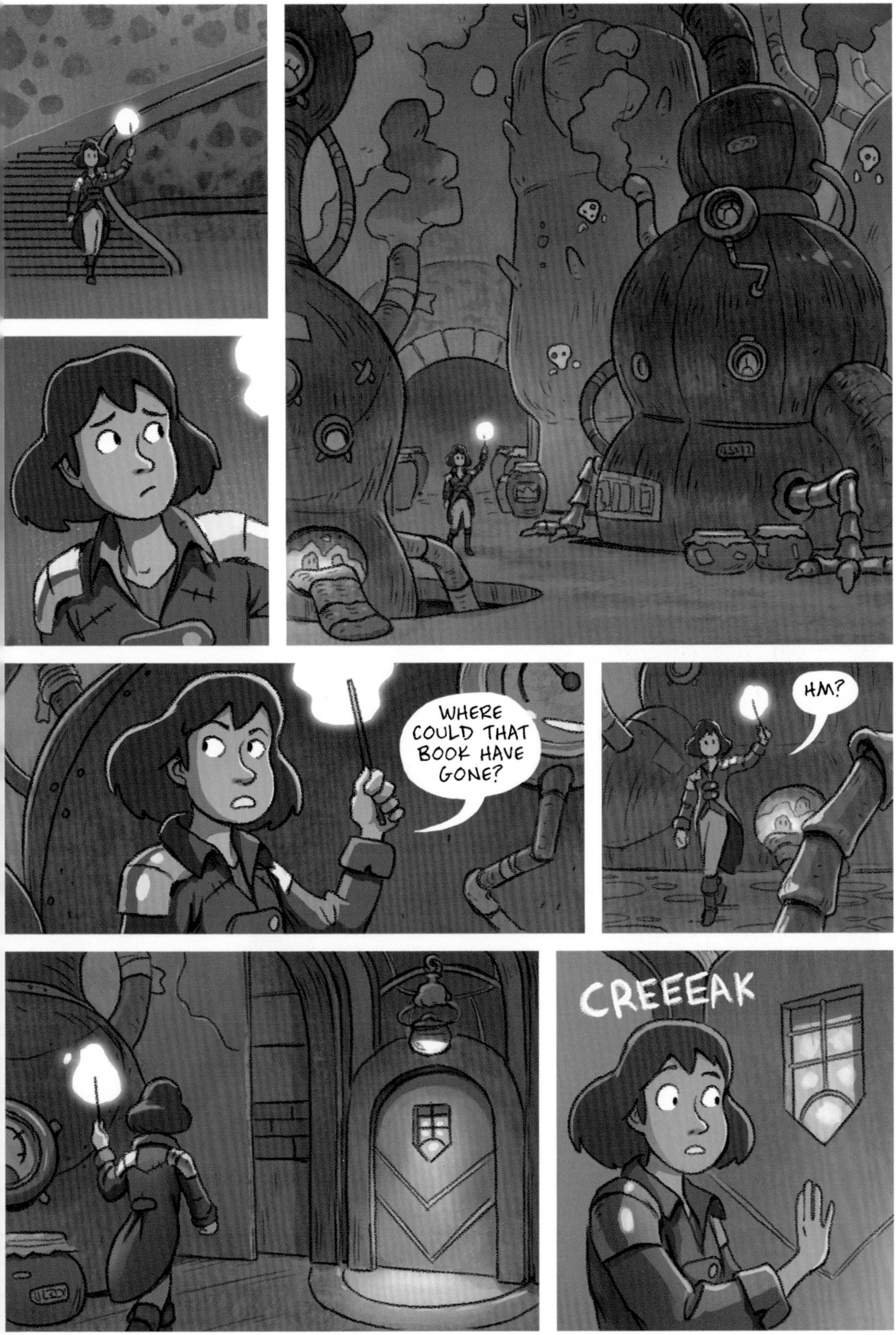
WHERE COULD THAT BOOK HAVE GONE?
HM?
CREEEAK

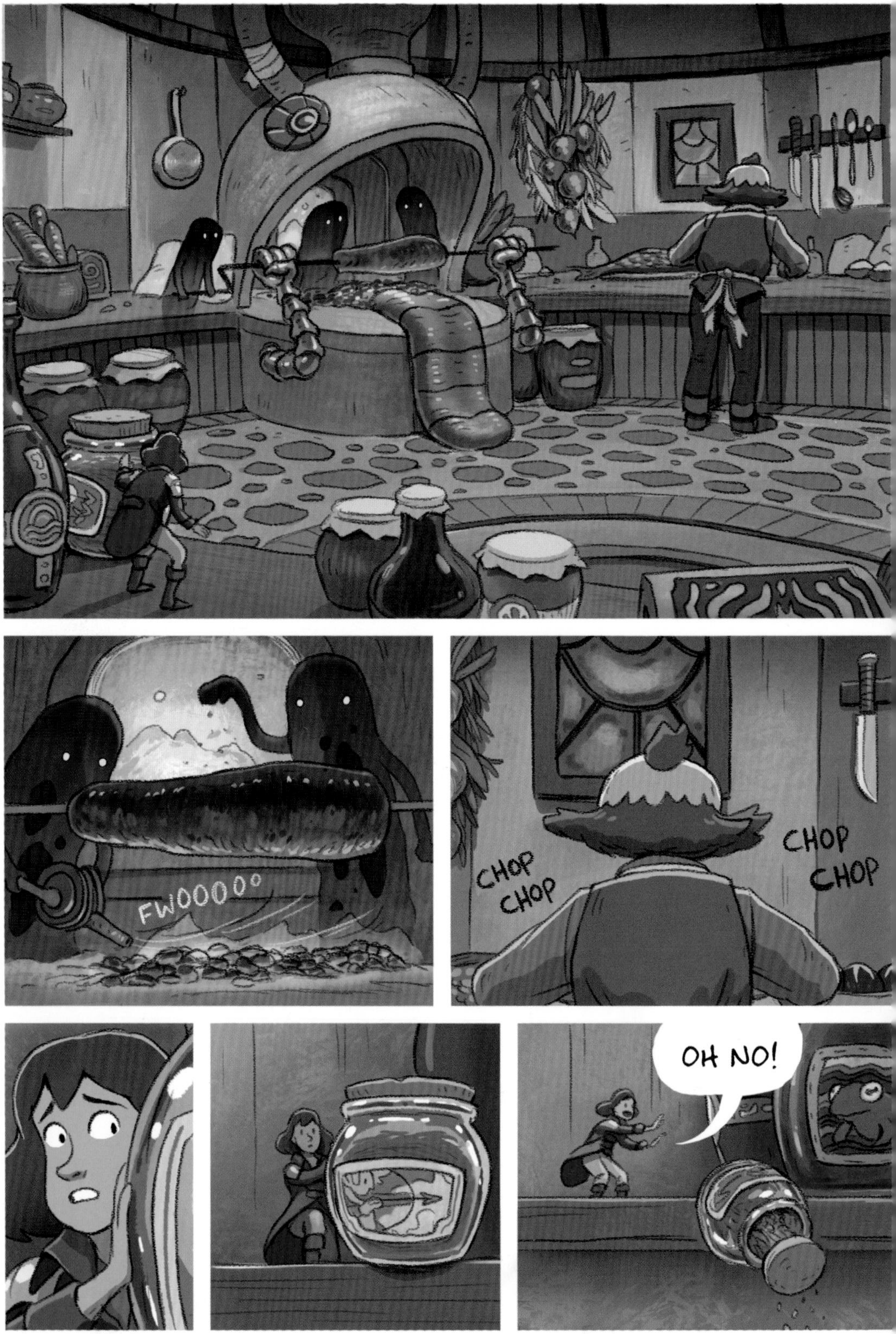
FWOOOOO
CHOP CHOP
CHOP CHOP
OH NO!

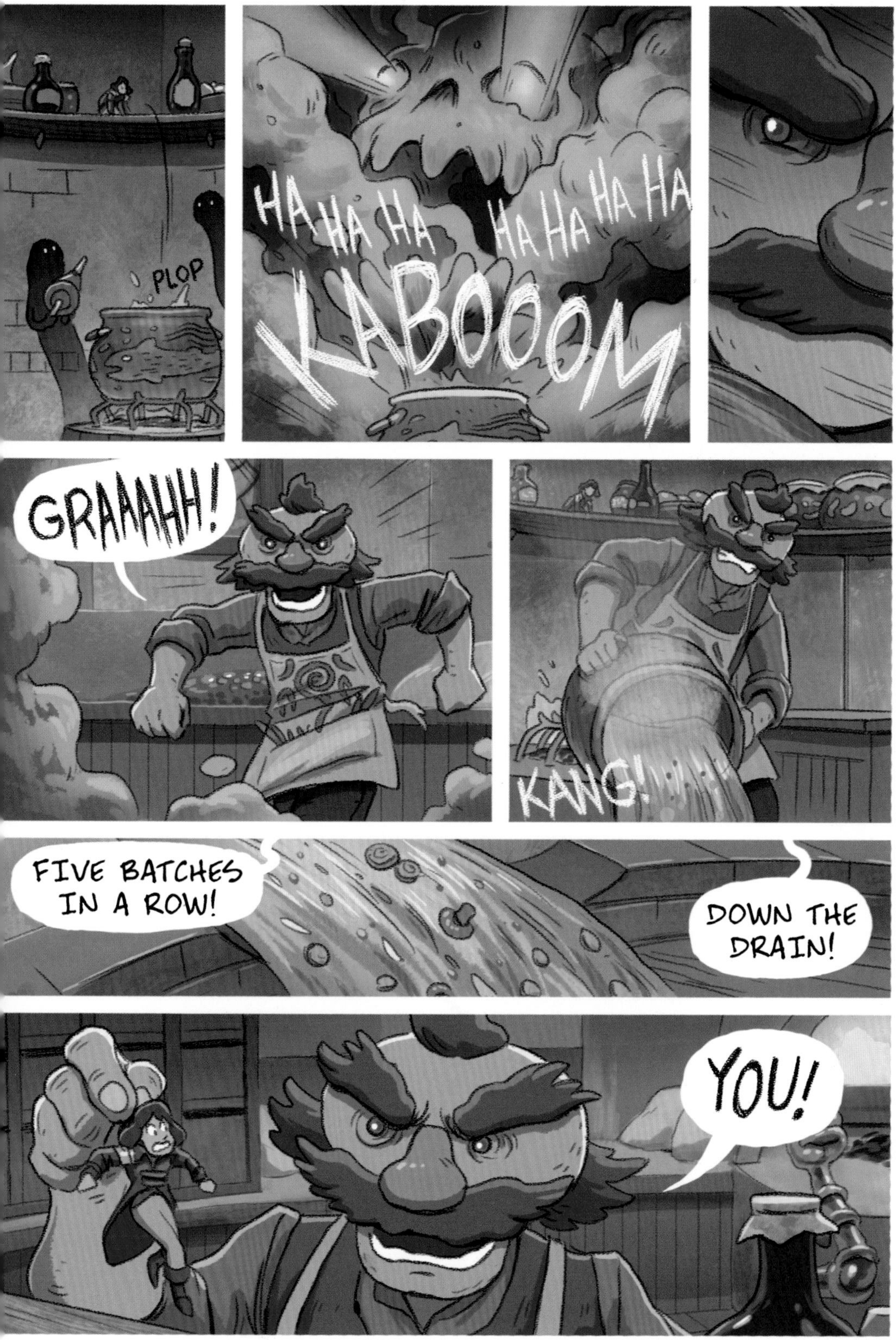
PLOP
HA HA HA HA HA HA HA HA
KABOOOM
GRAAAHH!
KANG!
FIVE BATCHES IN A ROW!
DOWN THE DRAIN!
YOU!

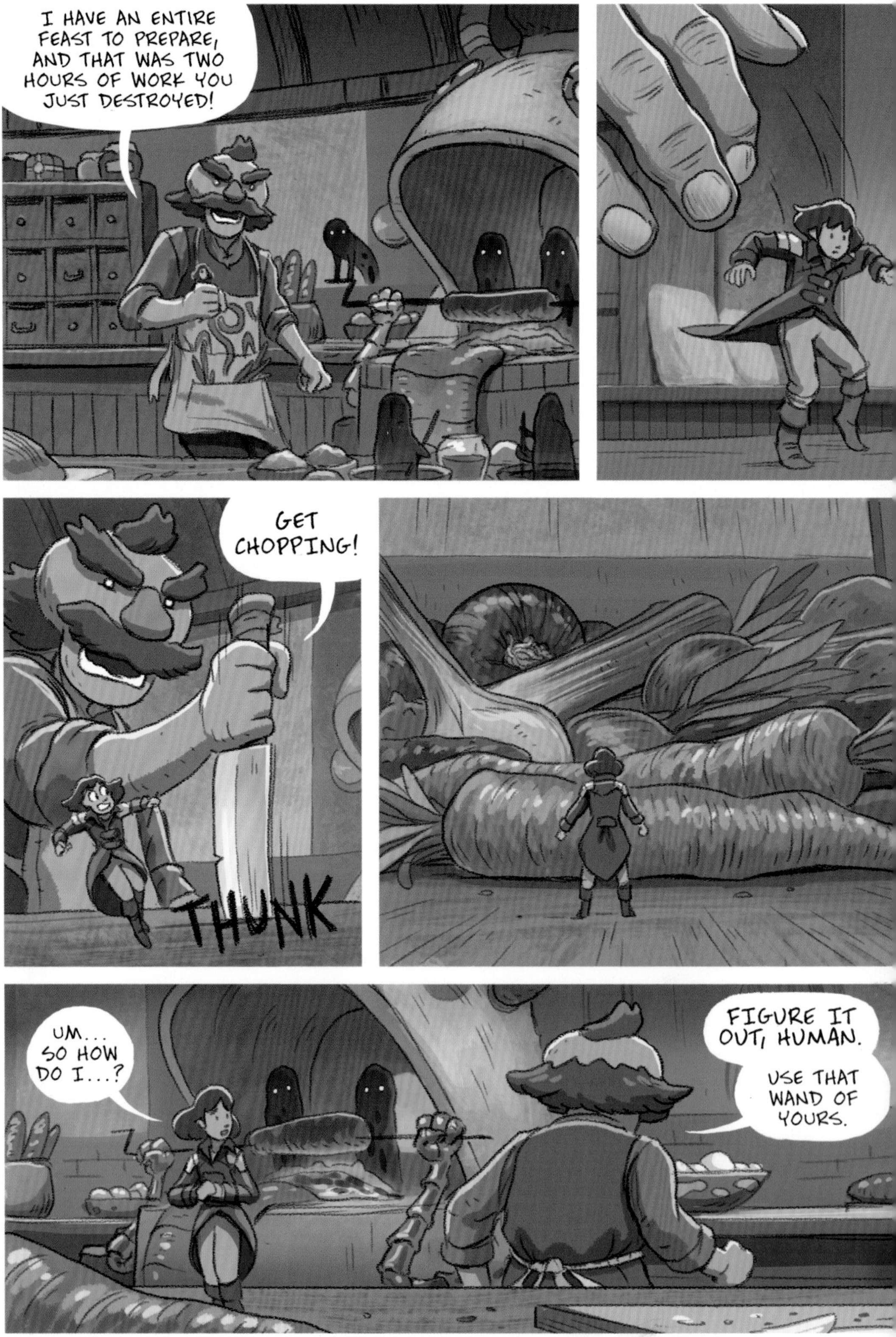
I HAVE AN ENTIRE FEAST TO PREPARE, AND THAT WAS TWO HOURS OF WORK YOU JUST DESTROYED!
GET CHOPPING!
THUNK
UM... SO HOW DO I...?
FIGURE IT OUT, HUMAN.
USE THAT WAND OF YOURS.

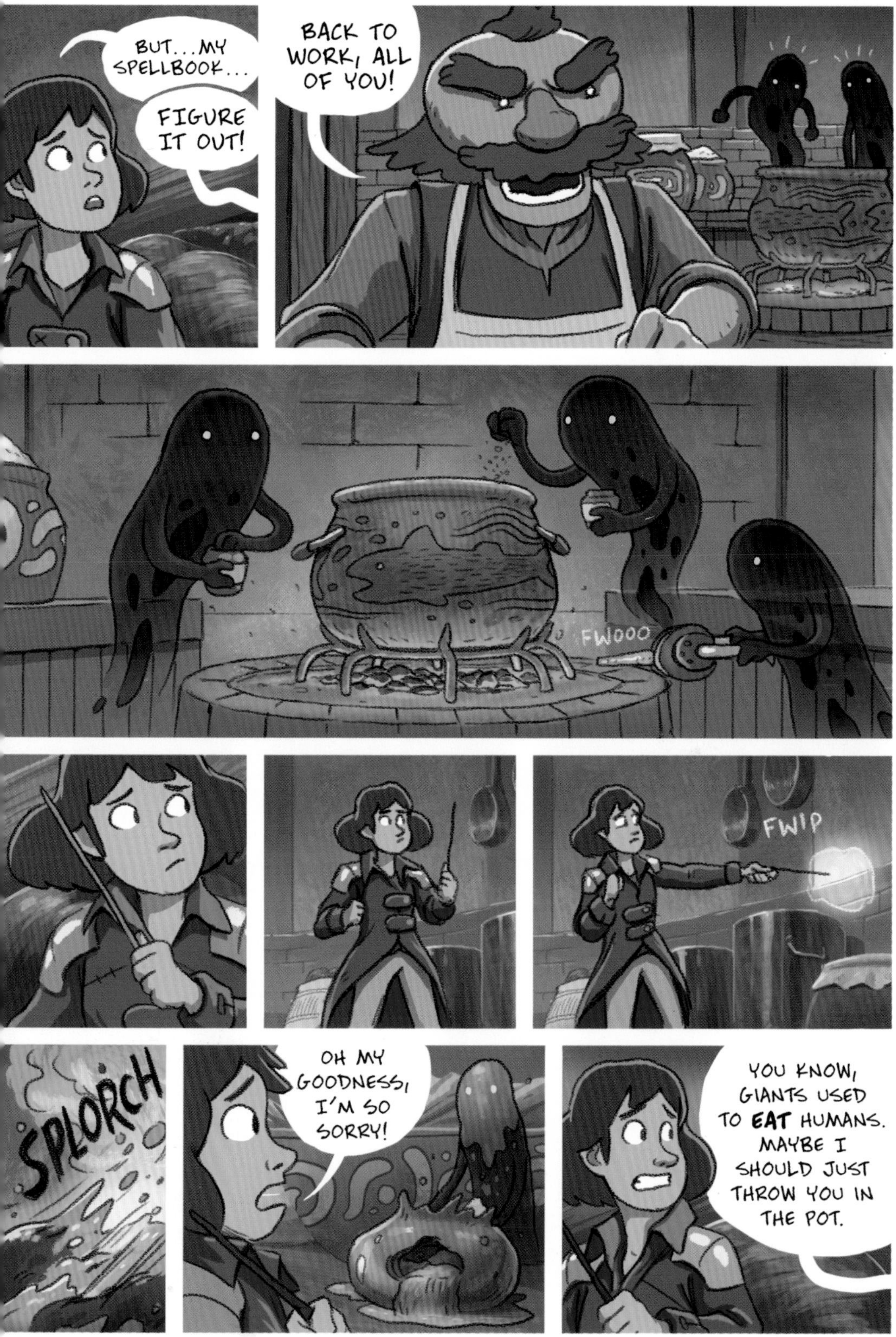
BUT...MY SPELLBOOK...
FIGURE IT OUT!
BACK TO WORK, ALL OF YOU!
FWOOO
FWIP
SPLORCH
OH MY GOODNESS, I'M SO SORRY!
YOU KNOW, GIANTS USED TO EAT HUMANS. MAYBE I SHOULD JUST THROW YOU IN THE POT.

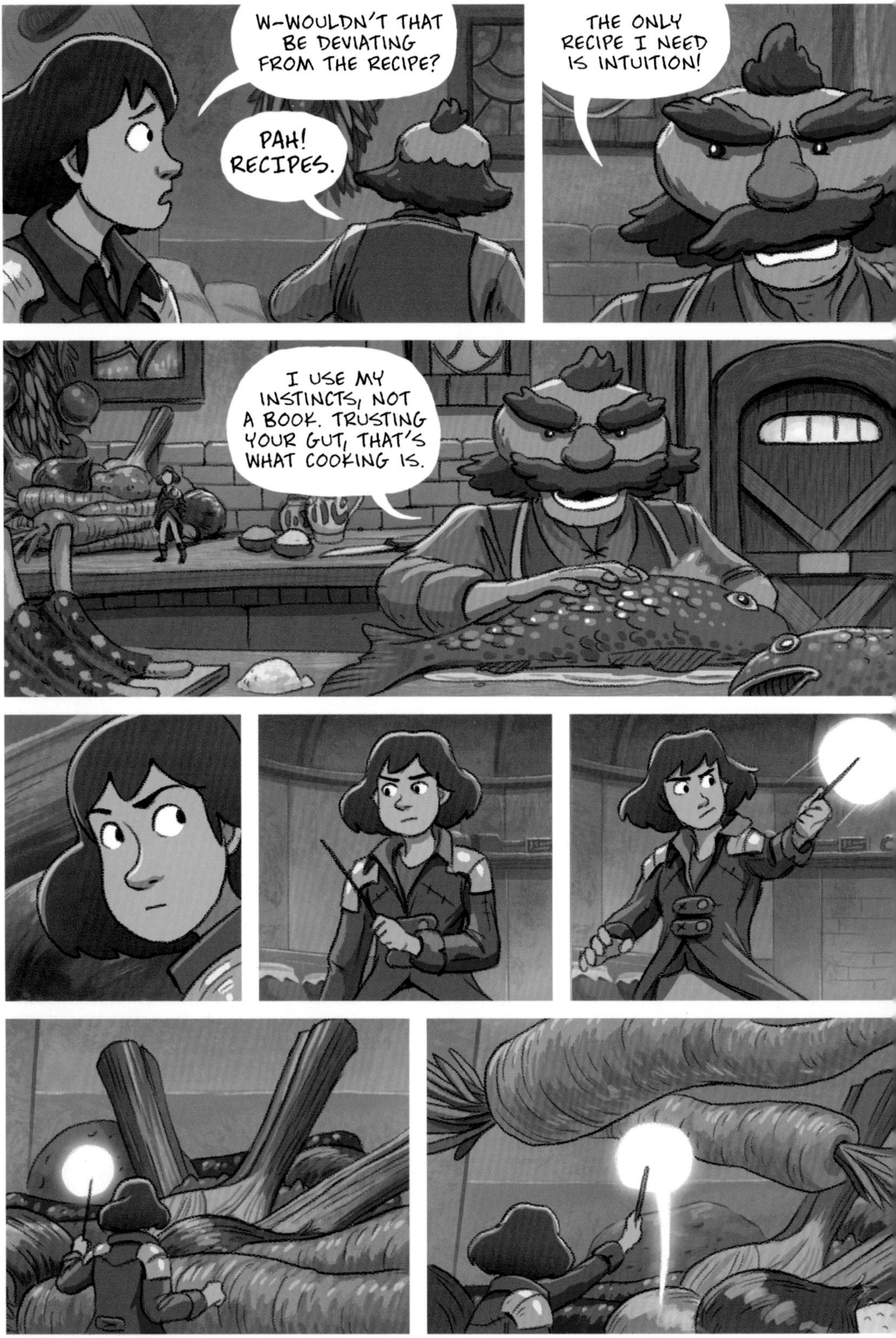
W-WOULDN'T THAT BE DEVIATING FROM THE RECIPE?
PAH! RECIPES.
THE ONLY RECIPE I NEED IS INTUITION!
I USE MY INSTINCTS, NOT A BOOK. TRUSTING YOUR GUT, THAT'S WHAT COOKING IS.

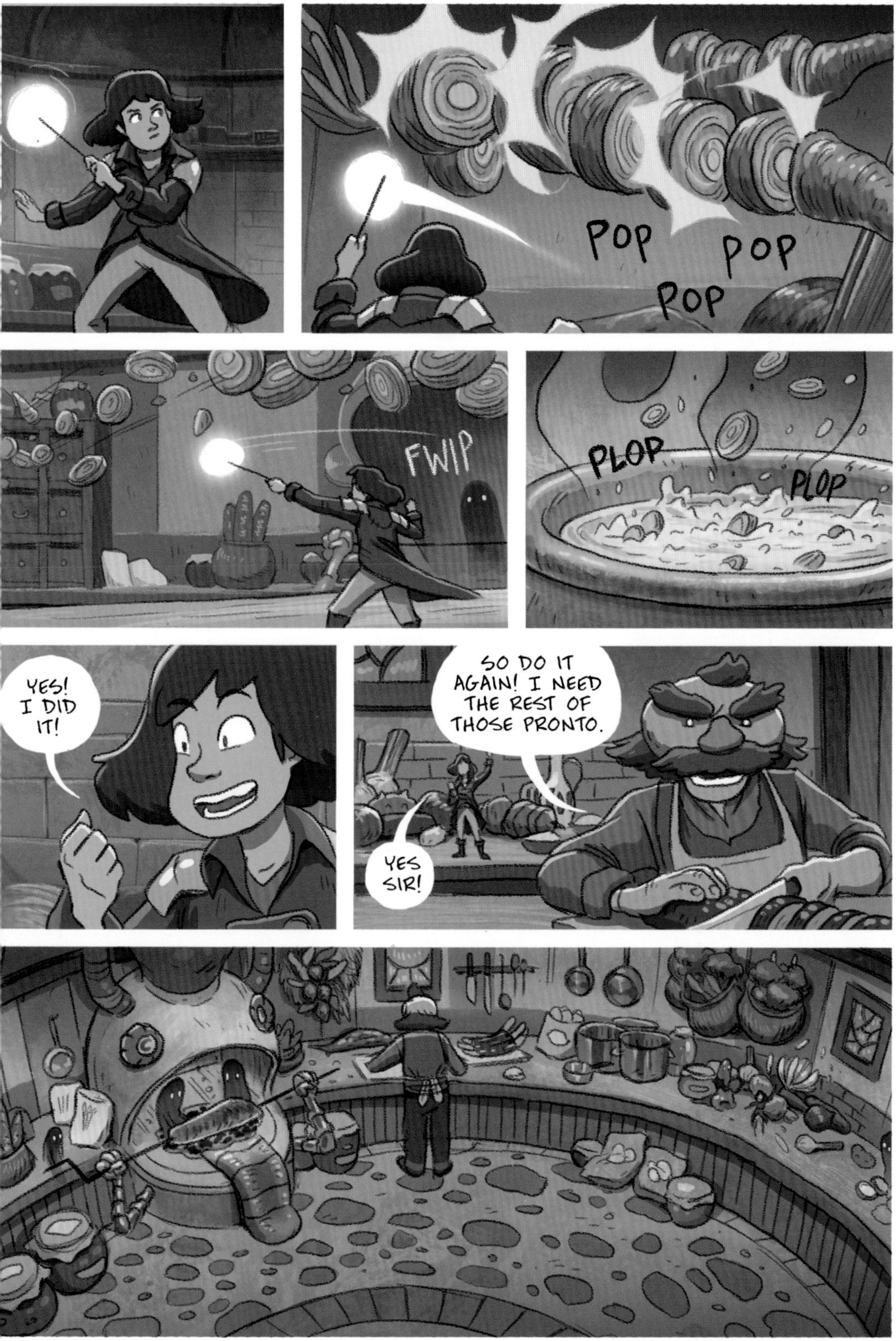
POP
POP
POP
FWIP
PLOP
PLOP
YES! I DID IT!
SO DO IT AGAIN! I NEED THE REST OF THOSE PRONTO.
YES SIR!

WOW, REALLY GOOD!

HMPH. YES, GOOD, BUT NOT GREAT.

IT LACKS DEPTH. VARIETY. PUNCH.

WHAT DO YOU THINK IT NEEDS?

I'M STILL NOT SURE. THIS IS MY SIXTH BATCH.

HMM, WHAT DID I KNOCK IN EARLIER?

ARROWSPICE? I DON'T KNOW WHY I KEEP IT AROUND. YOU SAW HOW VOLATILE IT CAN BE.

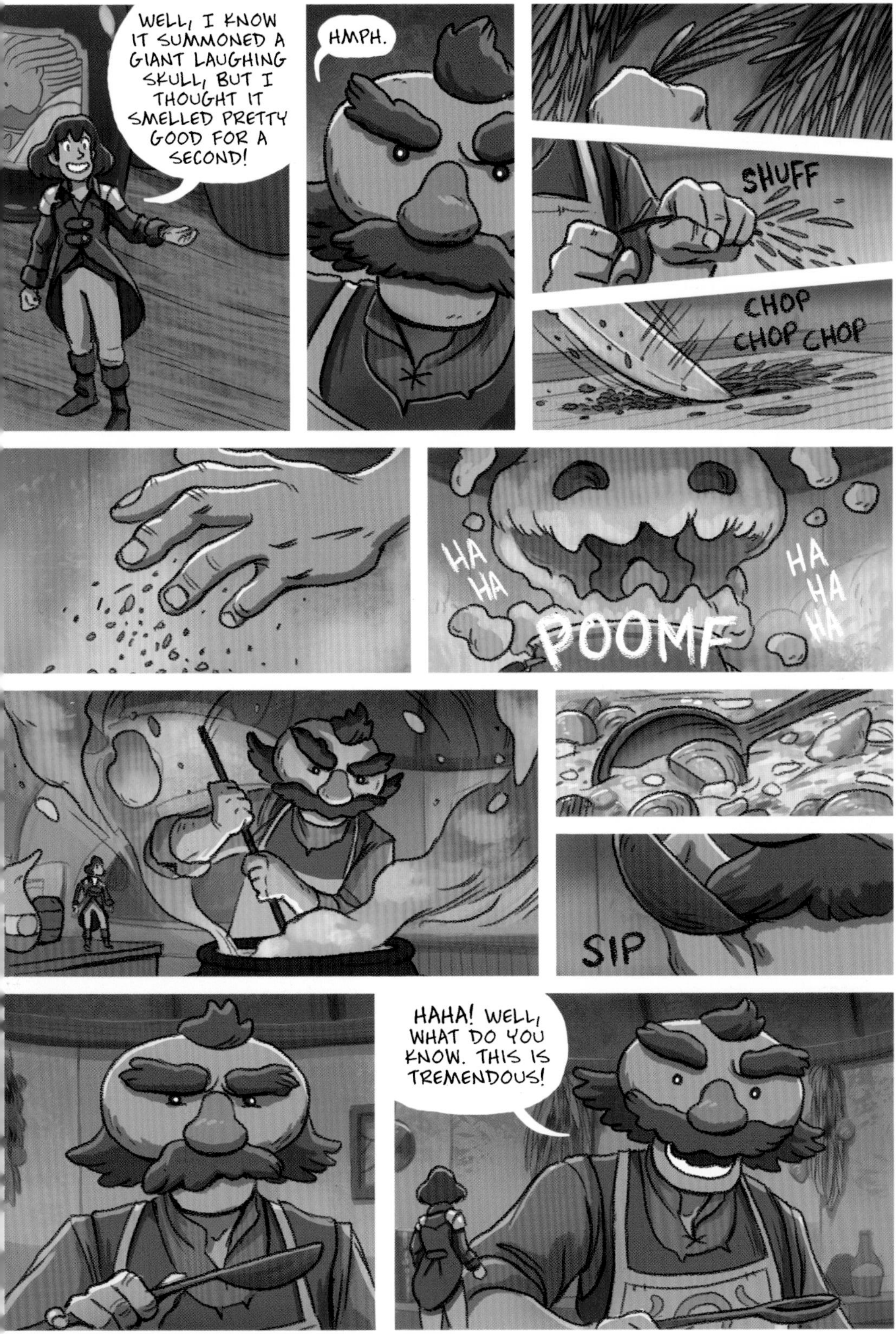

WELL, I KNOW IT SUMMONED A GIANT LAUGHING SKULL, BUT I THOUGHT IT SMELLED PRETTY GOOD FOR A SECOND!
HMPH.
SHUFF
CHOP CHOP CHOP
HA HA
HA HA HA
POOMF
SIP
HAHA! WELL, WHAT DO YOU KNOW. THIS IS TREMENDOUS!

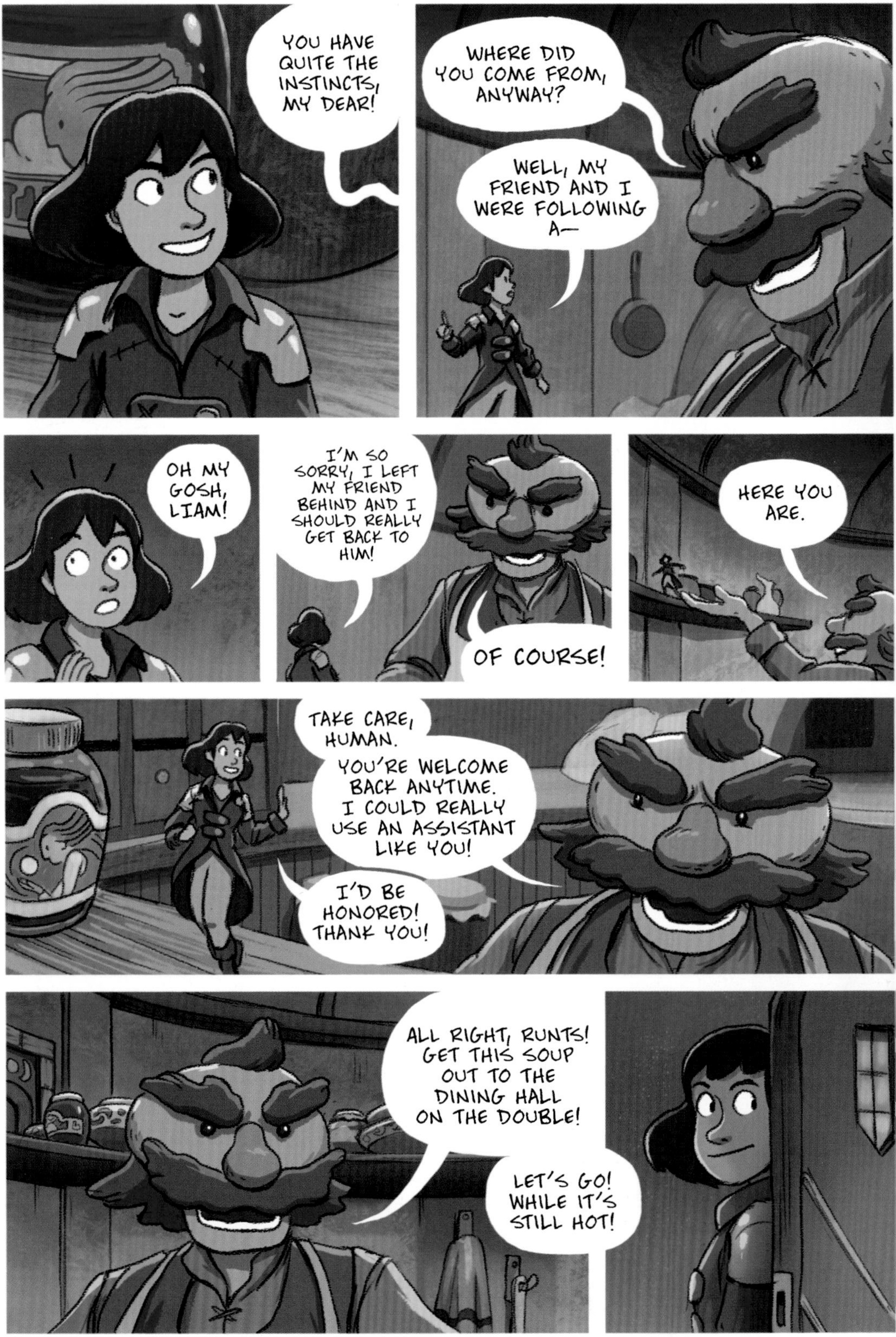
YOU HAVE QUITE THE INSTINCTS, MY DEAR!
WHERE DID YOU COME FROM, ANYWAY?
WELL, MY FRIEND AND I WERE FOLLOWING A—
OH MY GOSH, LIAM!
I'M SO SORRY, I LEFT MY FRIEND BEHIND AND I SHOULD REALLY GET BACK TO HIM!
OF COURSE!
HERE YOU ARE.
TAKE CARE, HUMAN.
YOU'RE WELCOME BACK ANYTIME. I COULD REALLY USE AN ASSISTANT LIKE YOU!
I'D BE HONORED! THANK YOU!
ALL RIGHT, RUNTS! GET THIS SOUP OUT TO THE DINING HALL ON THE DOUBLE!
LET'S GO! WHILE IT'S STILL HOT!

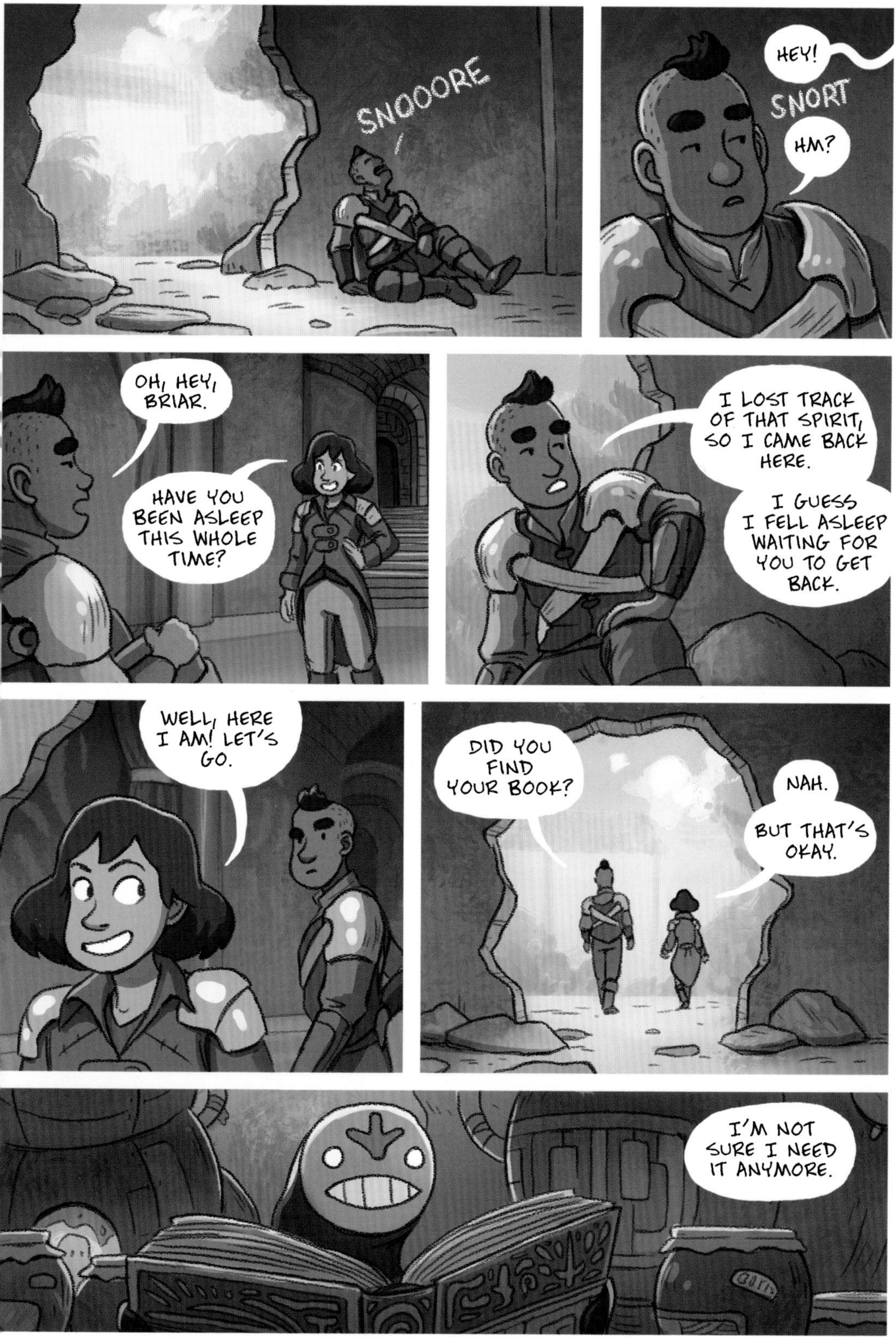
SNOOORE
HEY!
SNORT
HM?
OH, HEY, BRIAR.
HAVE YOU BEEN ASLEEP THIS WHOLE TIME?
I LOST TRACK OF THAT SPIRIT, SO I CAME BACK HERE.
I GUESS I FELL ASLEEP WAITING FOR YOU TO GET BACK.
WELL, HERE I AM! LET'S GO.
DID YOU FIND YOUR BOOK?
NAH.
BUT THAT'S OKAY.
I'M NOT SURE I NEED IT ANYMORE.

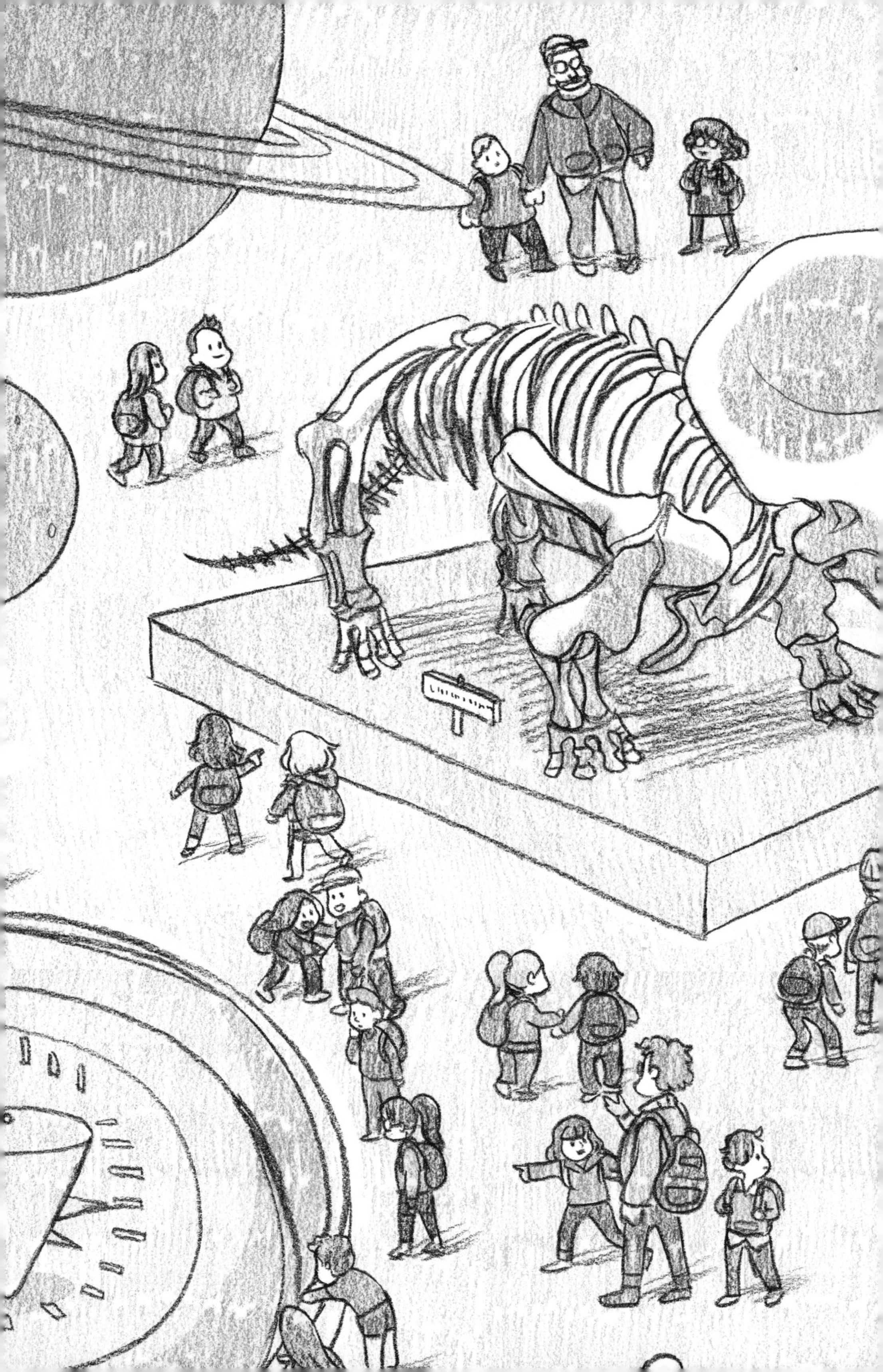

It probably started the time my dad
farted in front of everybody on our field trip
to the Science Academy.

It wasn't his fault! He has a condition, I swear!

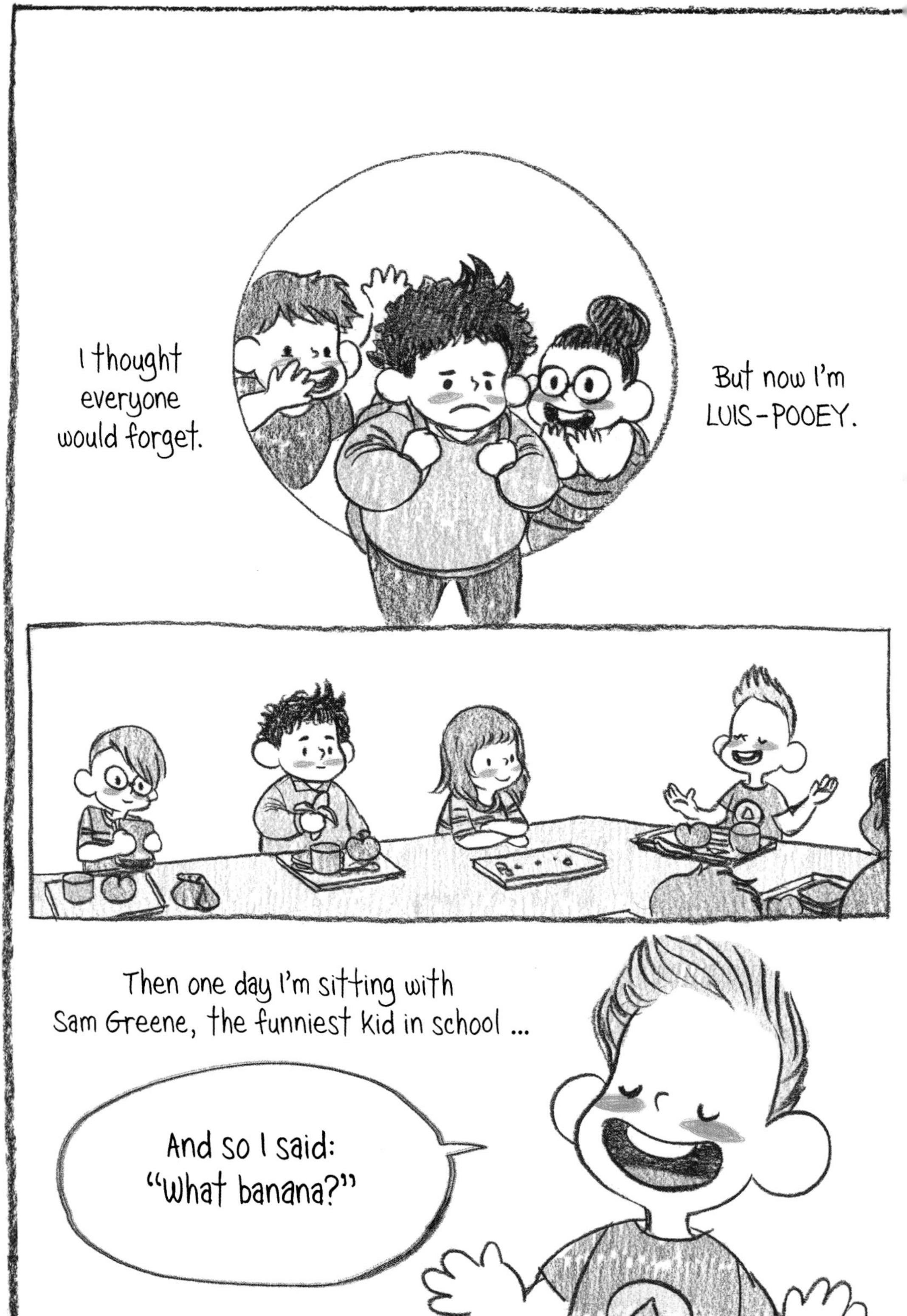
I thought everyone would forget.
But now I'm LUIS-POOEY.
Then one day I'm sitting with Sam Greene, the funniest kid in school ...
And so I said: "What banana?"

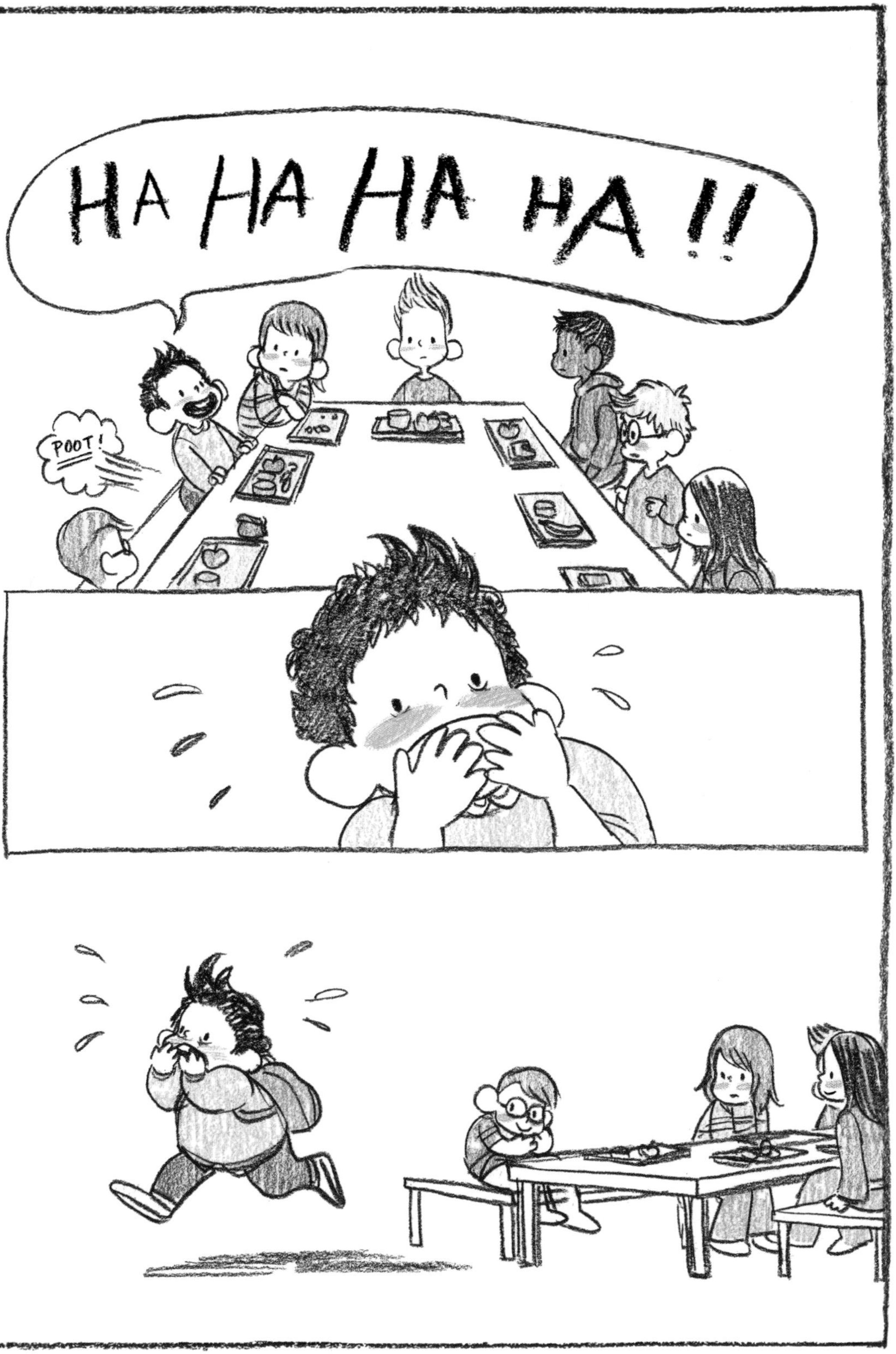
HA HA HA HA!!
POOT!

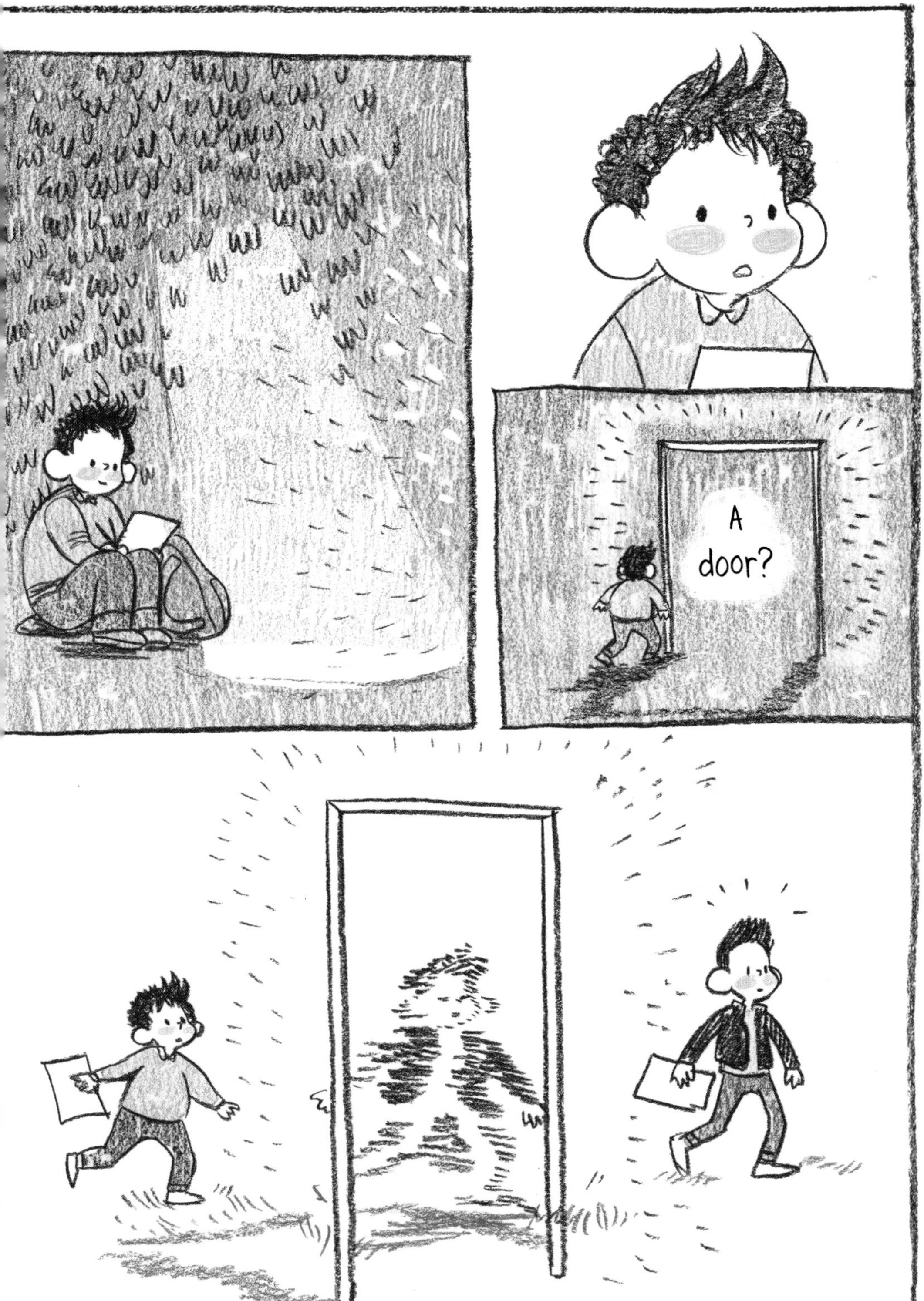
A door?

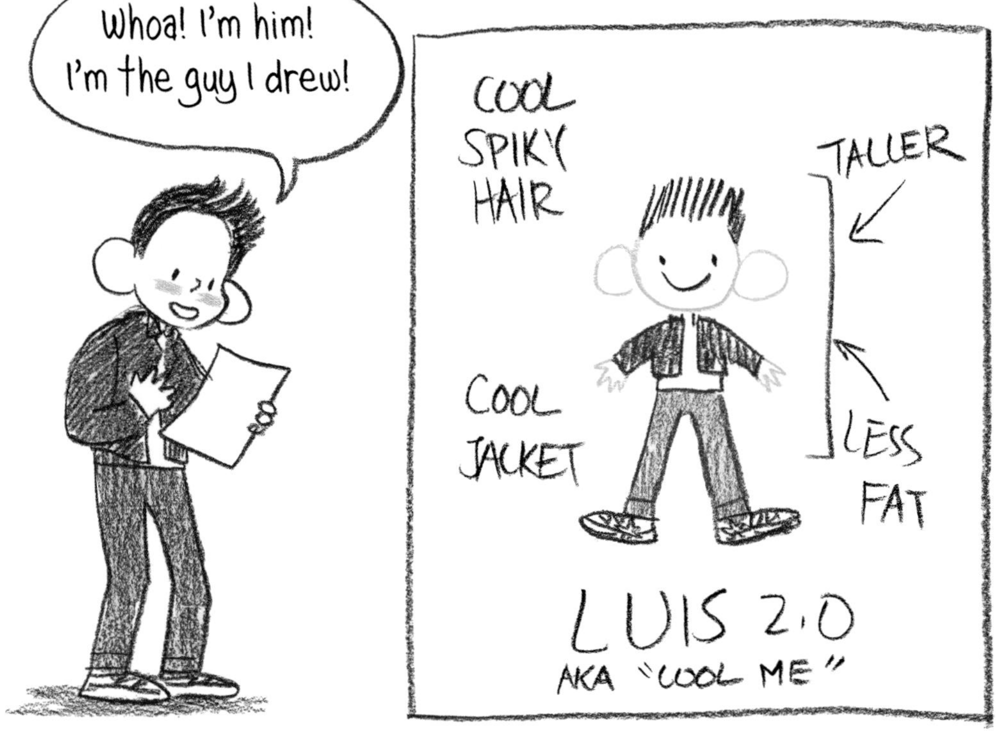
Whoa! I'm him!
I'm the guy I drew!
COOL SPIKY HAIR
TALLER
COOL JACKET
LESS FAT
LUIS 2.0
AKA "COOL ME"

I wondered if anyone would notice...

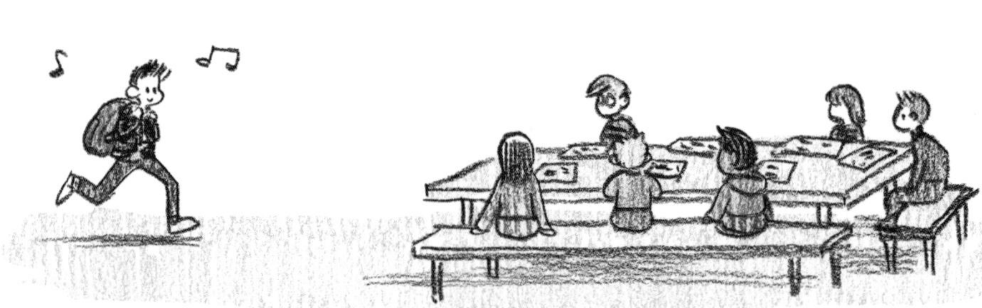

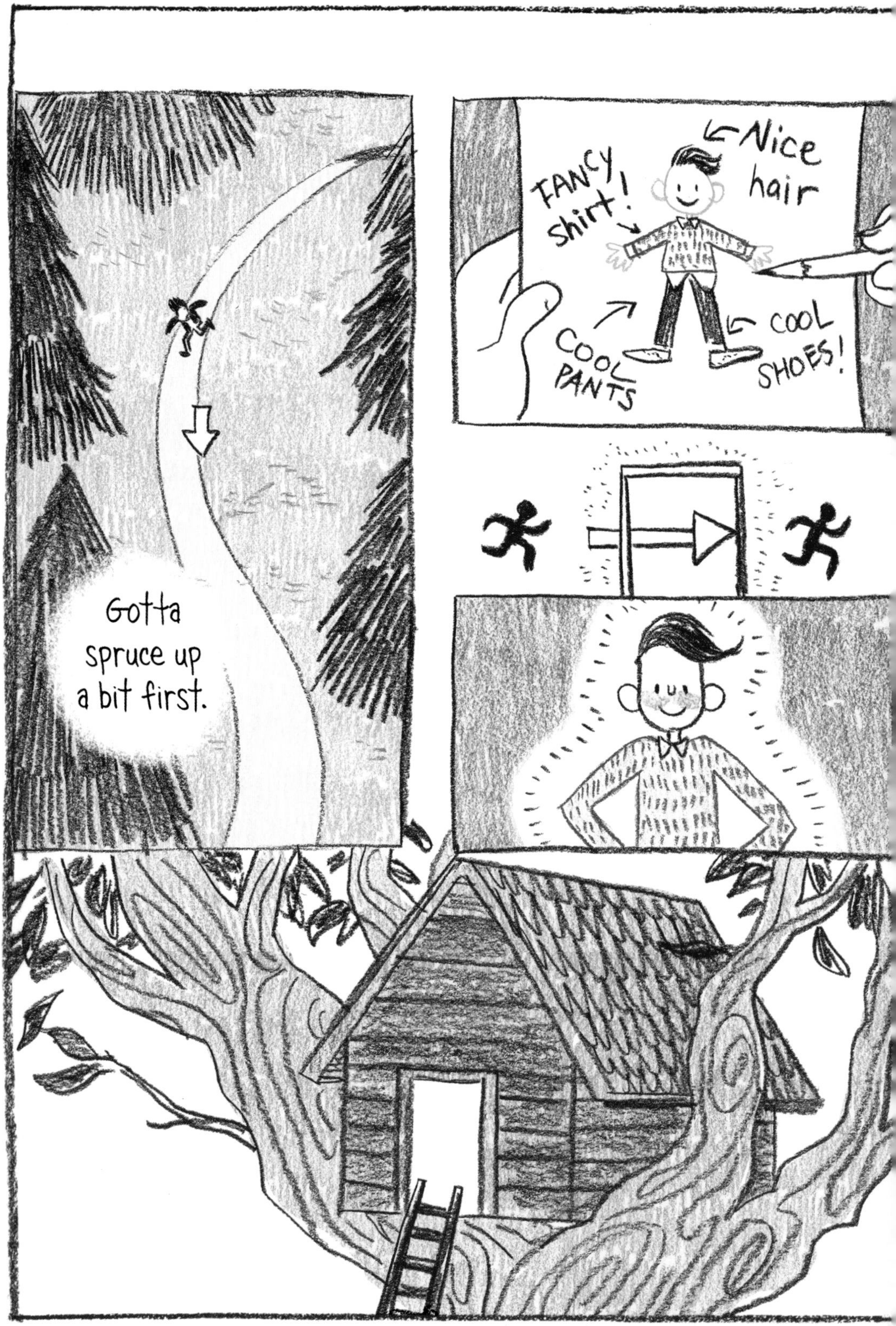
Gotta spruce up a bit first.
FANCY shirt!
Nice hair
COOL PANTS
COOL SHOES!

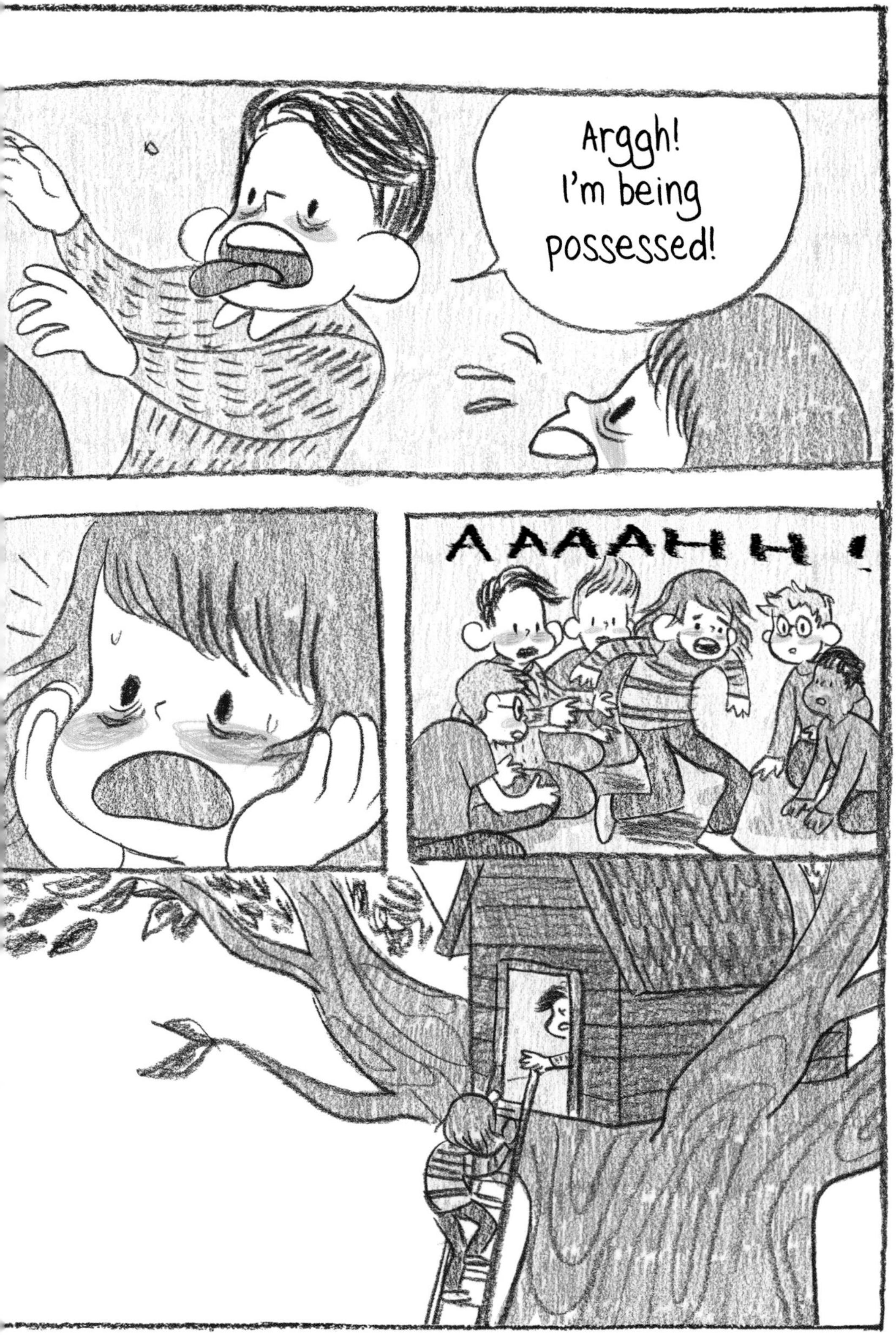
Arggh! I'm being possessed!
AAAAHH!

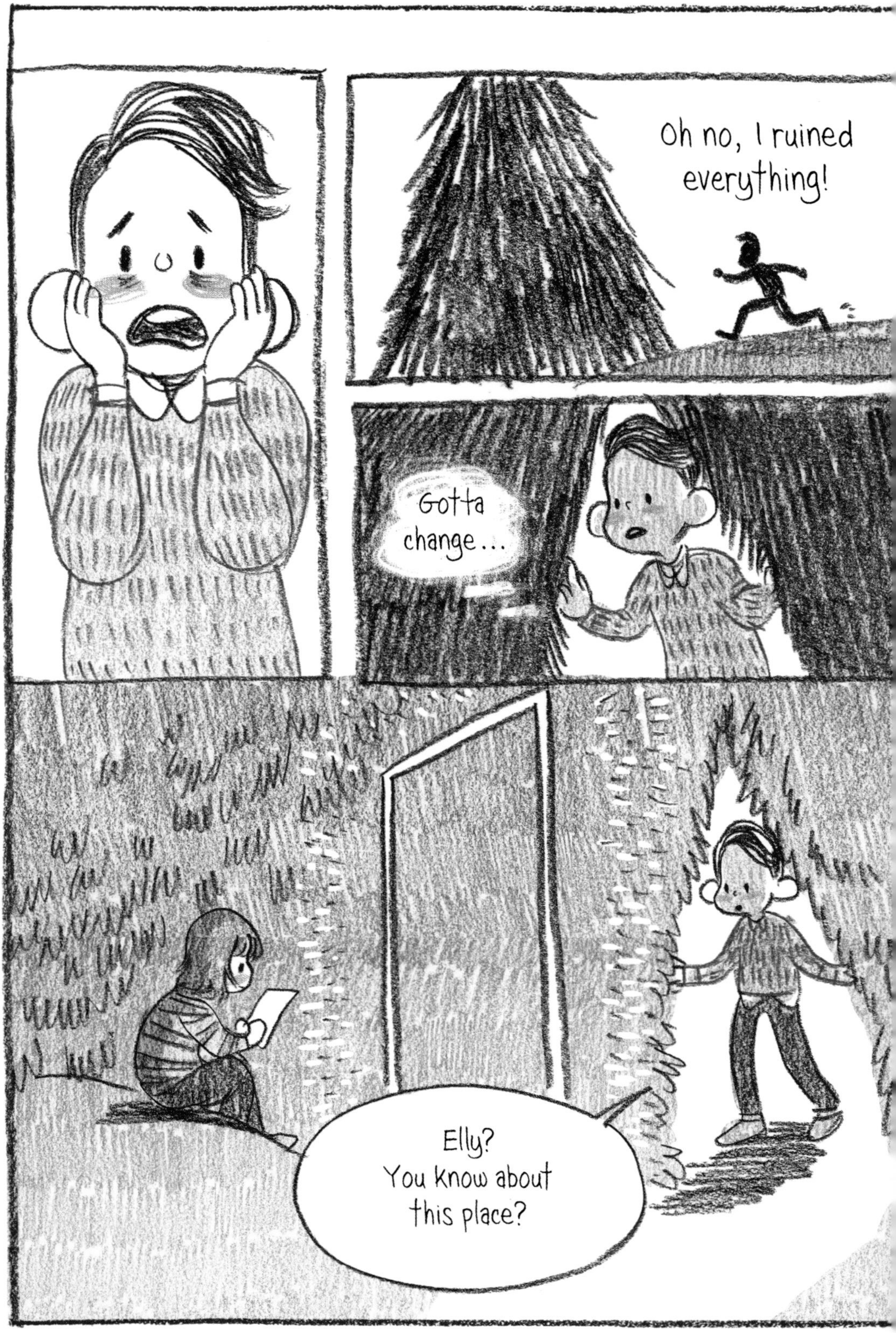
Oh no, I ruined everything!
Gotta change...
Elly? You know about this place?

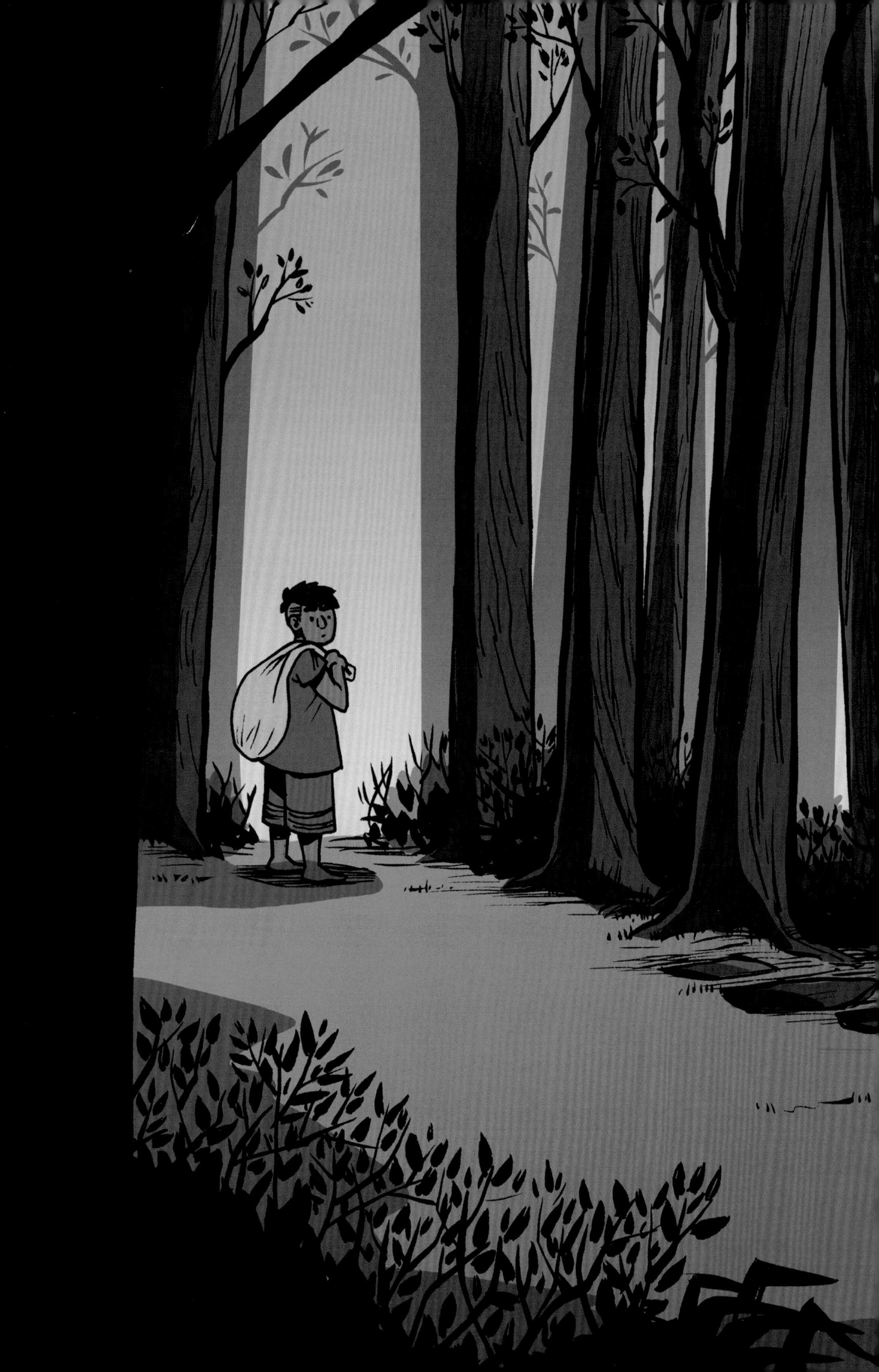

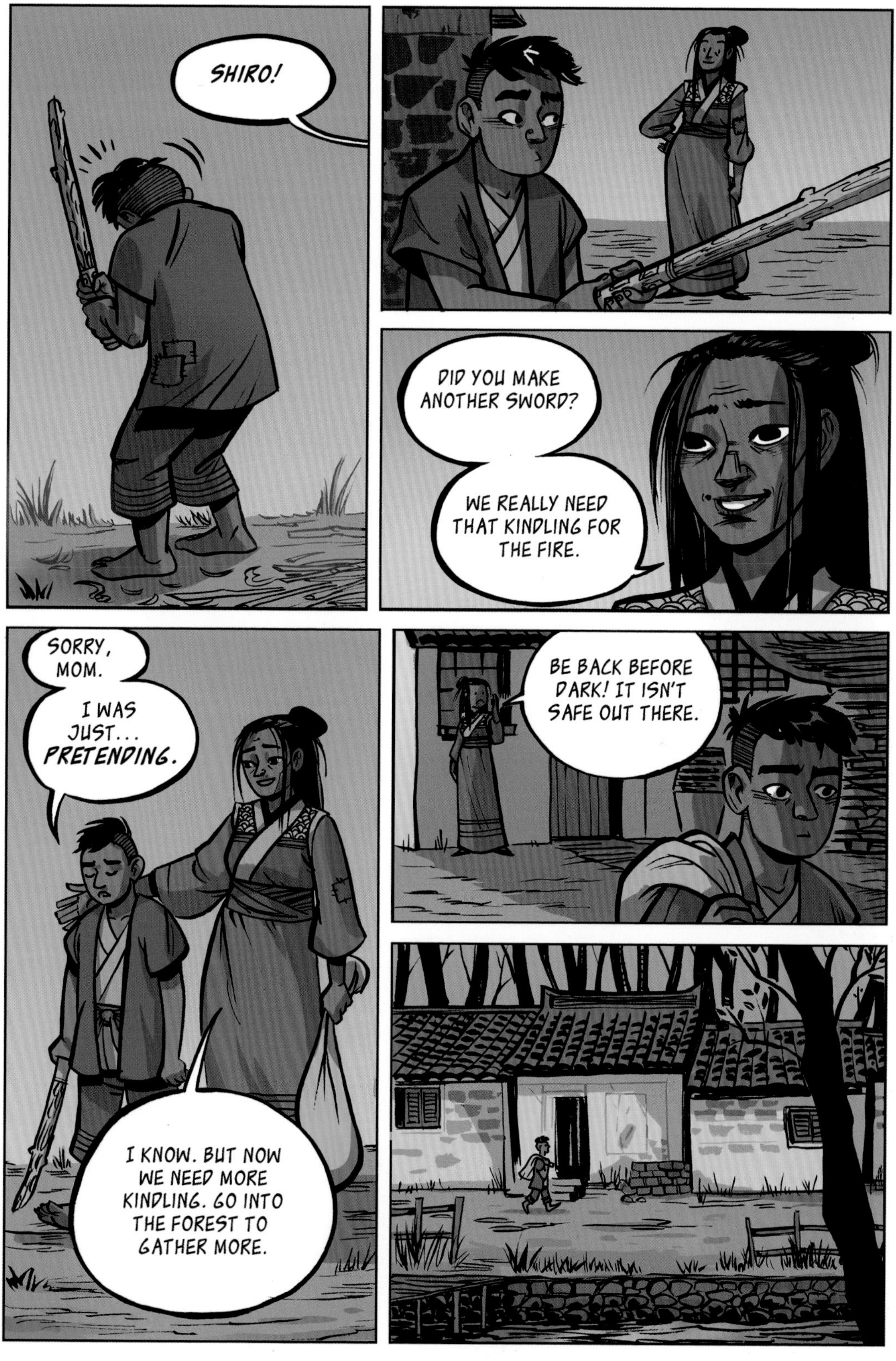
SHIRO!
DID YOU MAKE ANOTHER SWORD?
WE REALLY NEED THAT KINDLING FOR THE FIRE.
SORRY, MOM.
I WAS JUST... PRETENDING.
I KNOW. BUT NOW WE NEED MORE KINDLING. GO INTO THE FOREST TO GATHER MORE.
BE BACK BEFORE DARK! IT ISN'T SAFE OUT THERE.

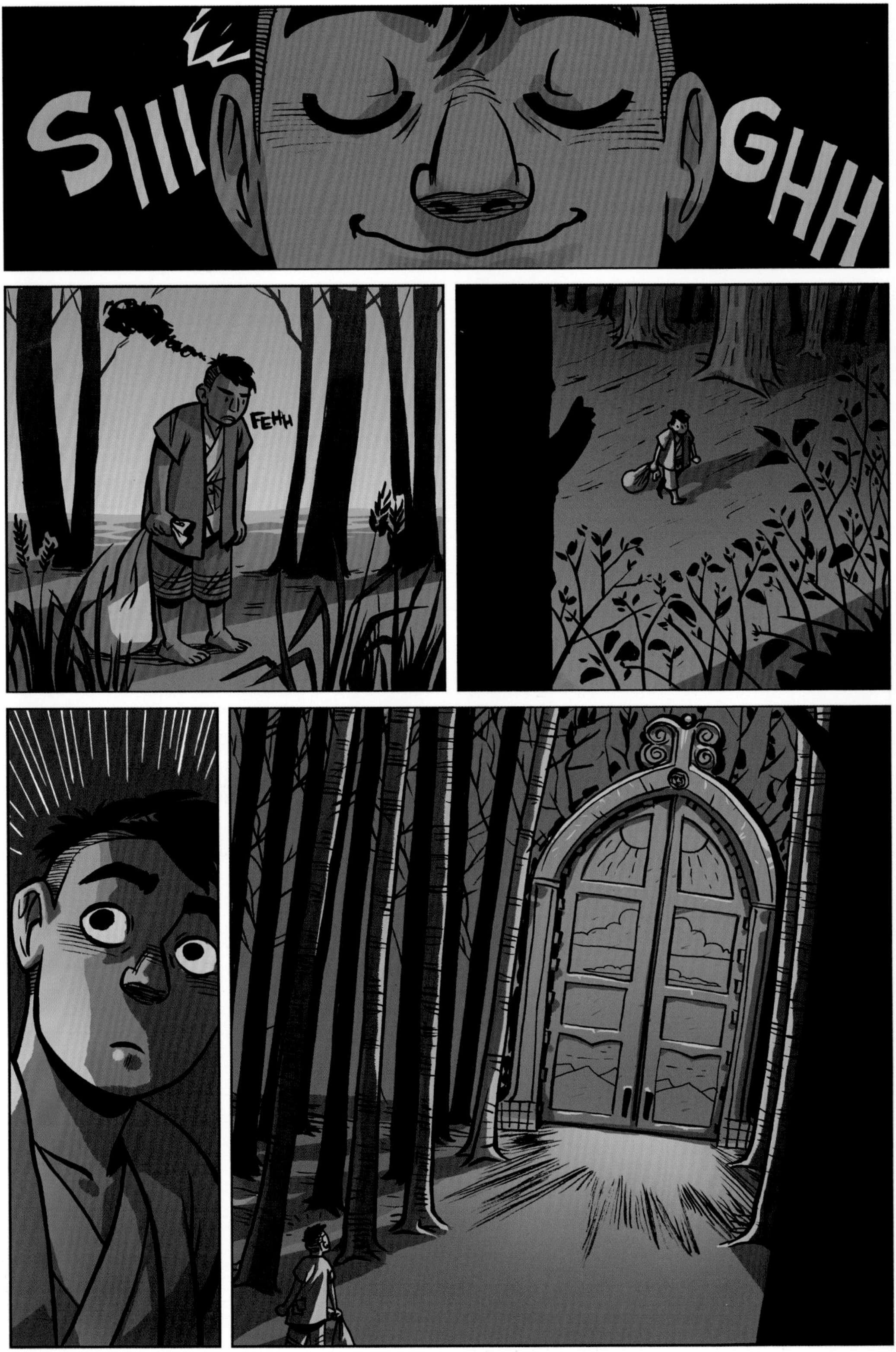
SIIIGHH
FEHH

GET OUT OF MY SIGHT! ALL YOU DO IS CAUSE TROUBLE!

SNIFF
SNIFF
SNIFF

UM...

YOUR NAME'S MISA, RIGHT?

SNIFF

HEH.

UM, MISA? YOU'RE A GIRL, RIGHT?

UMM ... WOULD YOU LIKE TO ... UM, COME OVER TO MY HOUSE FOR SUPPER? I PROMISE WE DON'T EAT STICKS.

OKAY.

I'M REALLY HAPPY TO SEE SHIRO FINALLY INVITING HIS FRIENDS OVER FOR SUPPER. IT'S USUALLY ONLY THE TWO OF US.

SCARF MUNCH CHOMP GOBBLE

BURRRPP

GOODNESS! WHAT AN APPETITE YOU HAVE, MISA.

IF YOU TWO ARE FINISHED, WHY DON'T YOU PLAY IN SHIRO'S ROOM?

PSHEW! YOU DIED!

ARRGHHH NOOOO!

BLAM! MAGIC!

YOUR TOYS ARE REALLY COOL.

OH, THANKS. MY MOM AND I MADE THEM.

YOUR MOM MADE YOU THESE?

SOME OF THEM. AND I MADE SOME. SHE TAUGHT ME HOW TO CARVE.

IF I COULD CARVE AWESOME THINGS LIKE THESE, I'D SHOW THEM TO EVERYBODY.

WHOS!

HEY, LET'S GO TO THE FOREST.

BUT IT'S AFTER DARK. WE'RE NOT SUPPOSED TO GO THERE AFTER DARK.

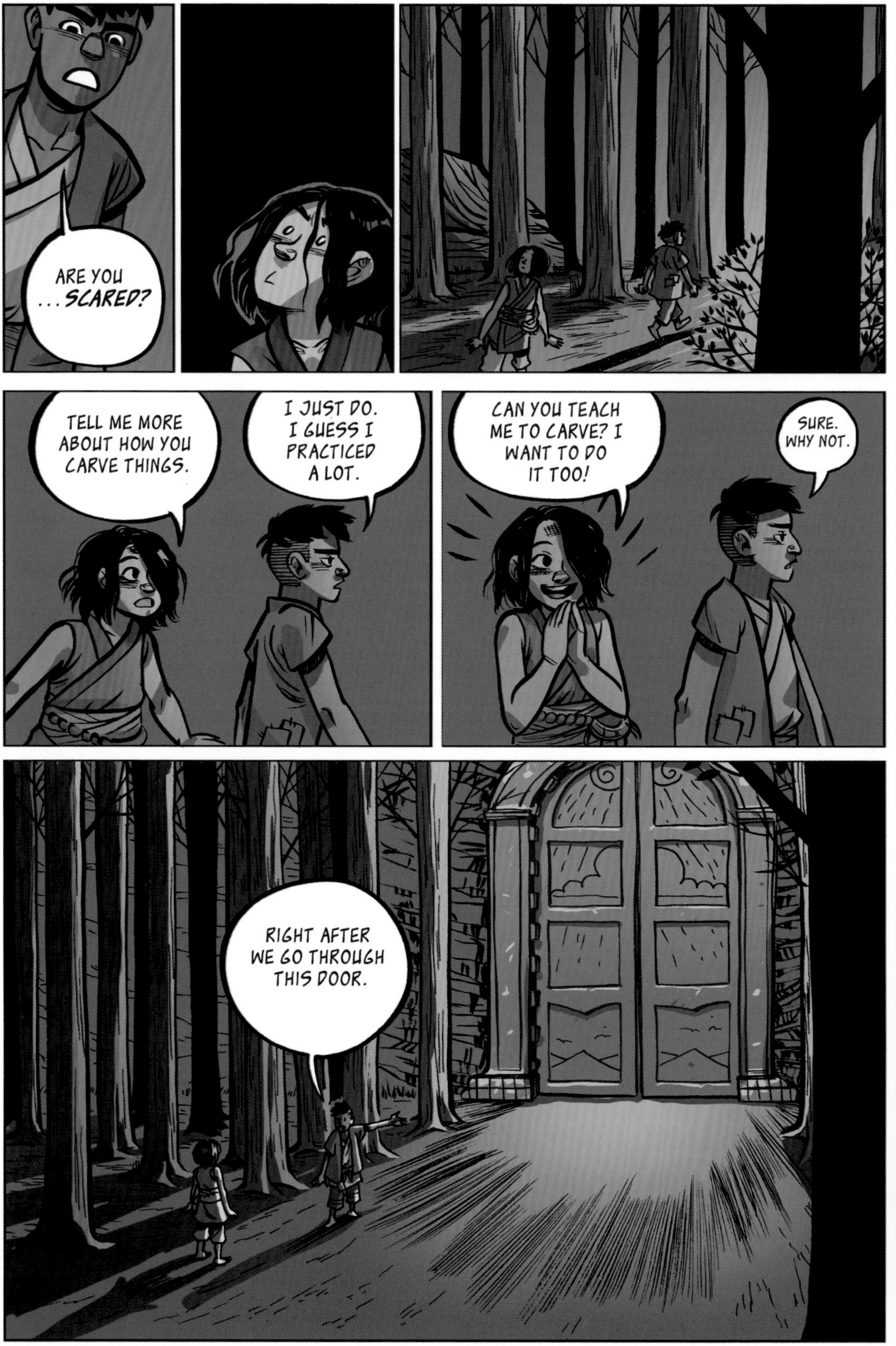
ARE YOU ...SCARED?
TELL ME MORE ABOUT HOW YOU CARVE THINGS.
I JUST DO. I GUESS I PRACTICED A LOT.
CAN YOU TEACH ME TO CARVE? I WANT TO DO IT TOO!
SURE. WHY NOT.
RIGHT AFTER WE GO THROUGH THIS DOOR.

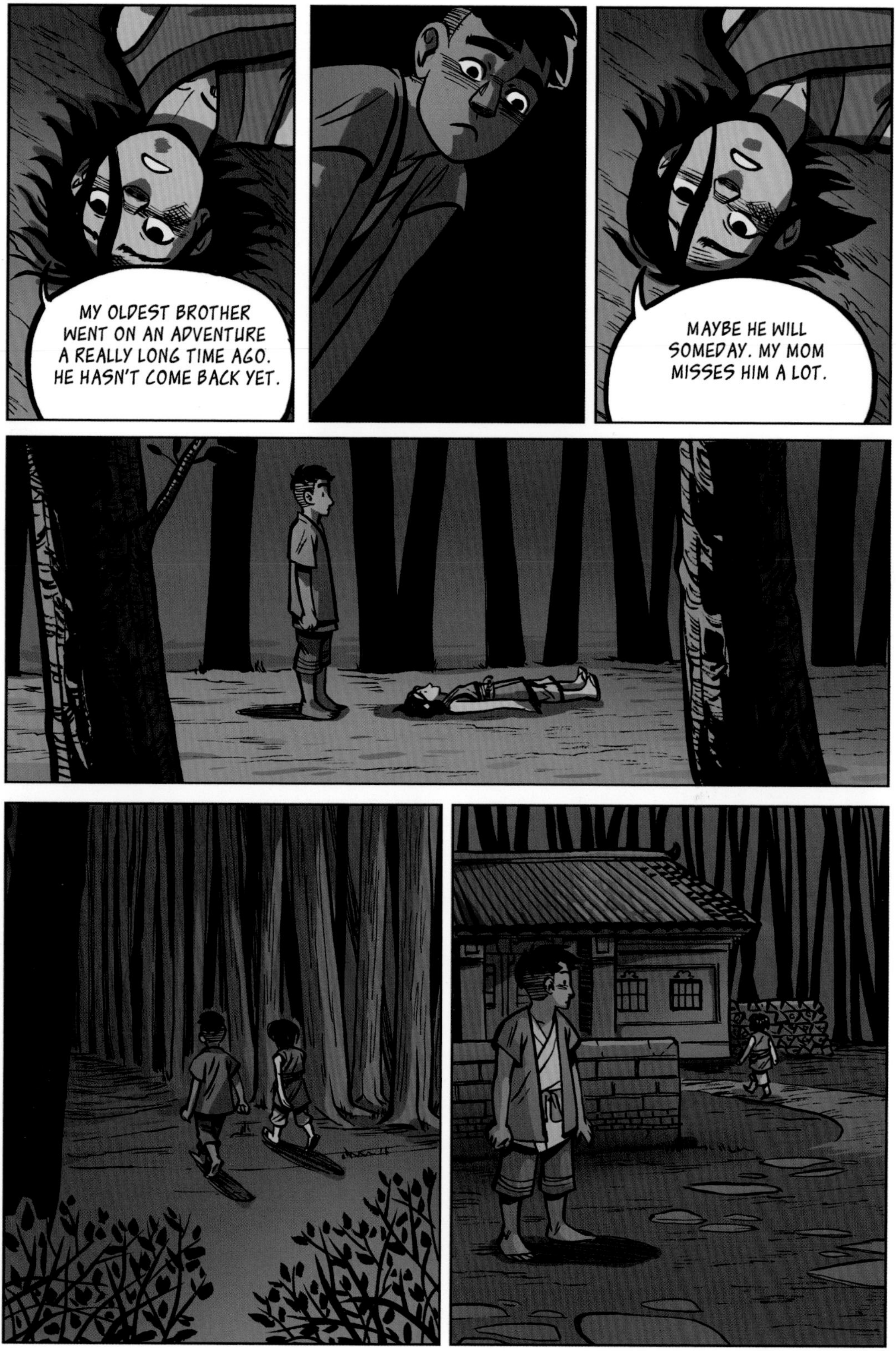
MY OLDEST BROTHER WENT ON AN ADVENTURE A REALLY LONG TIME AGO. HE HASN'T COME BACK YET.
MAYBE HE WILL SOMEDAY. MY MOM MISSES HIM A LOT.

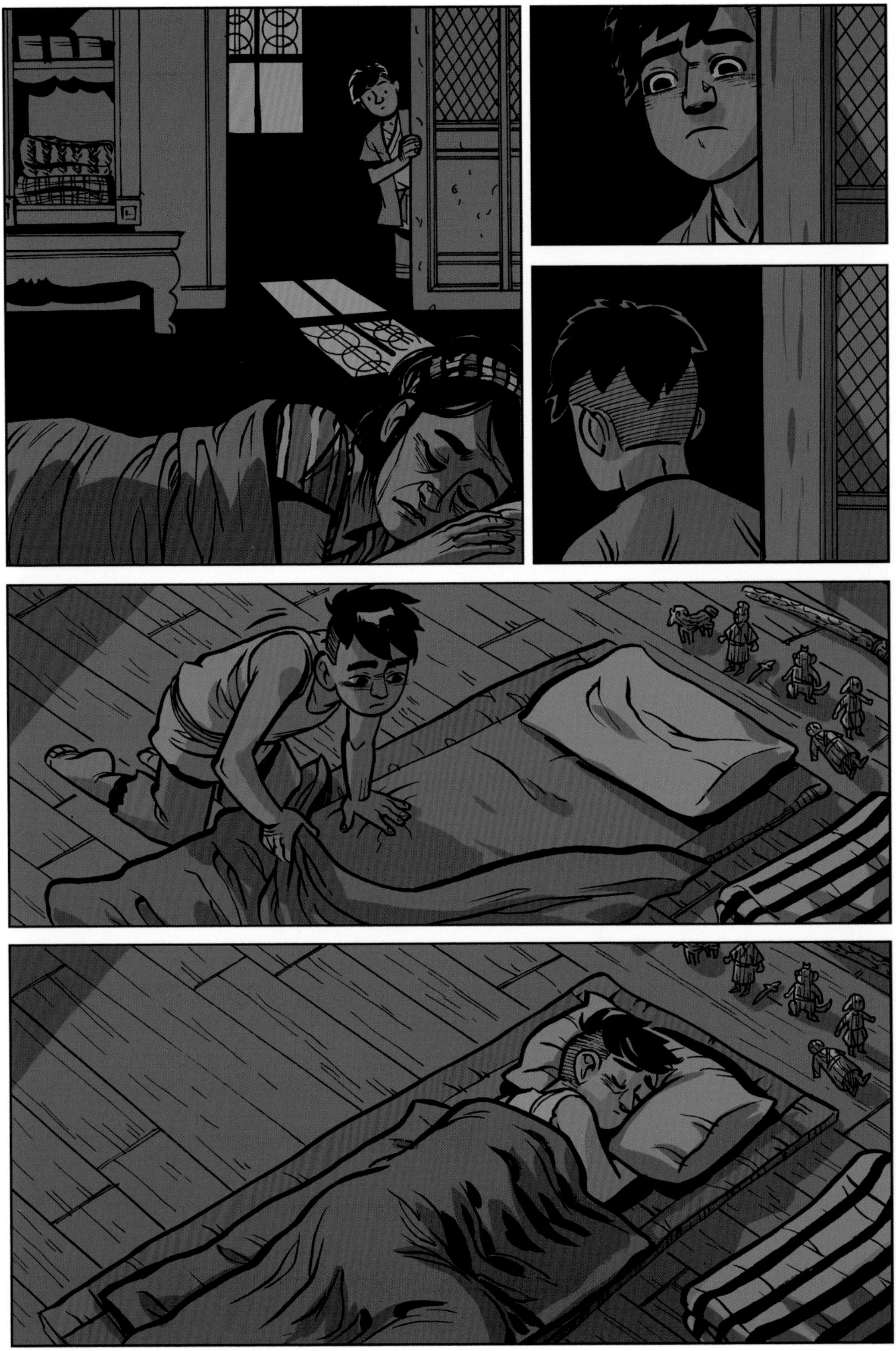

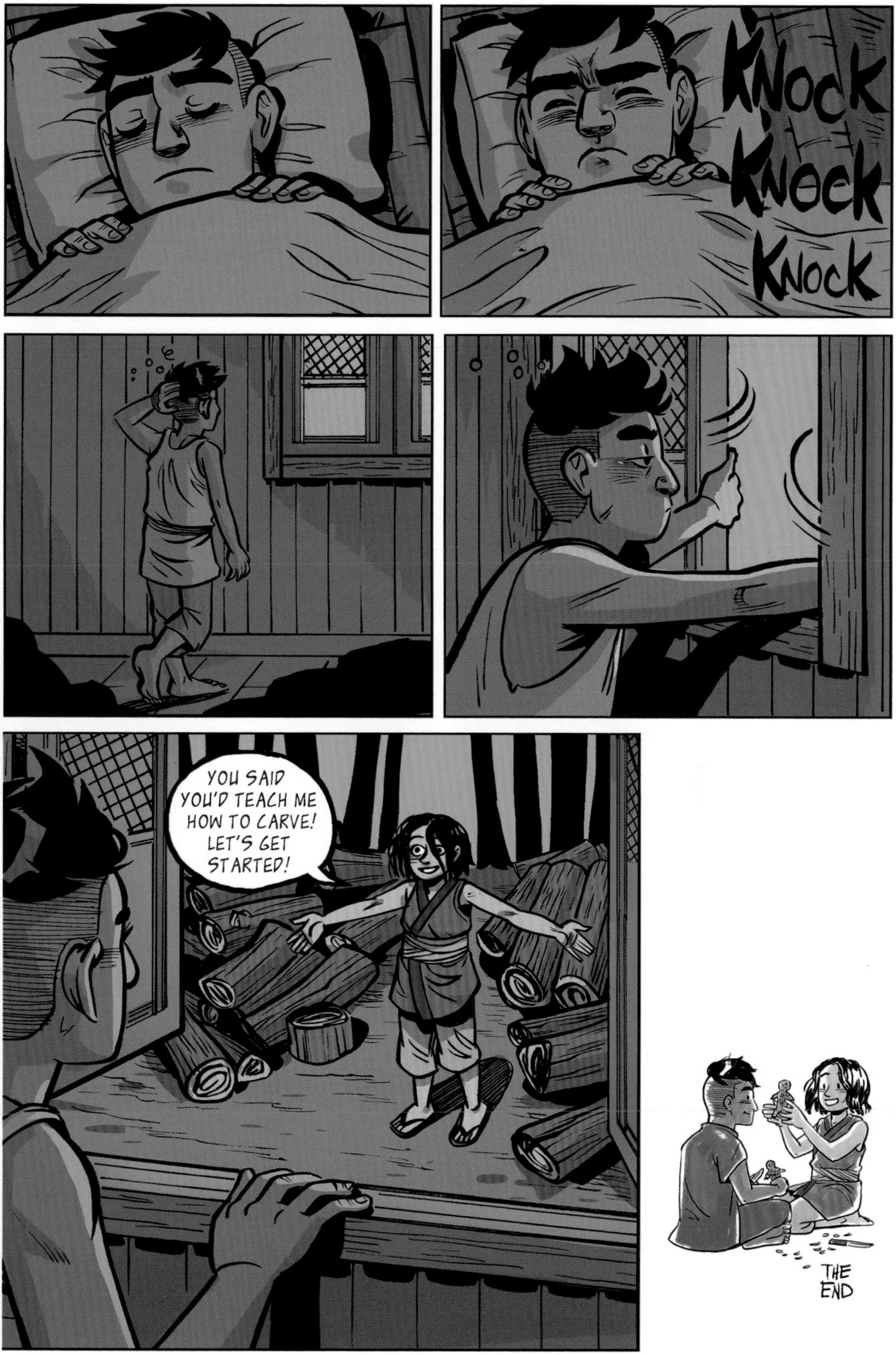
KNOCK
KNOCK
KNOCK
YOU SAID YOU'D TEACH ME HOW TO CARVE! LET'S GET STARTED!
THE END

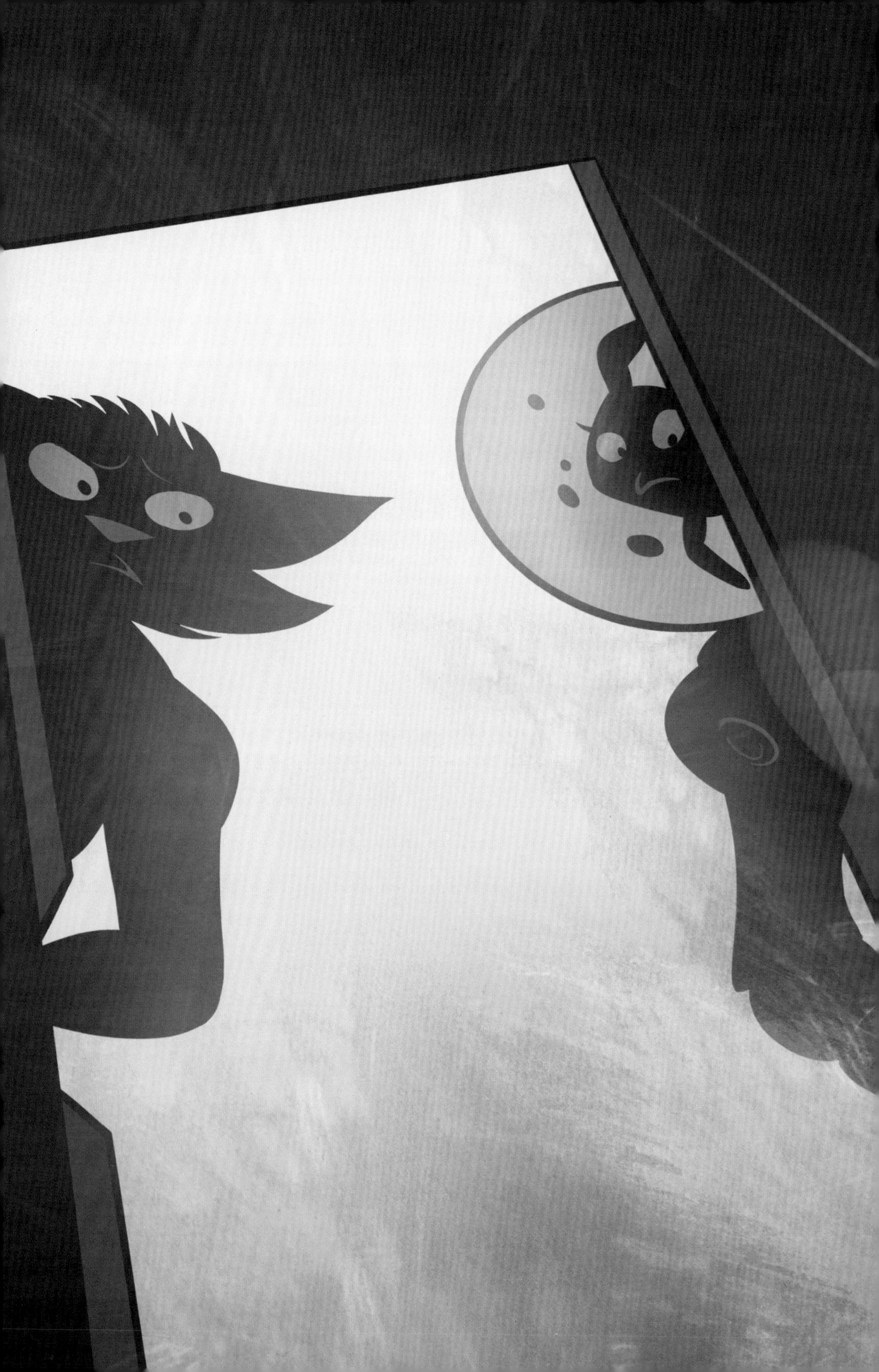

Fish N Chips

in
spring cleaning

BY STEVE HAMAKER

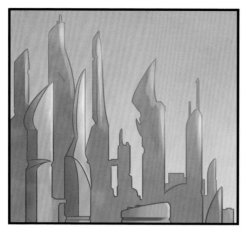

JAXER, TELL ME AGAIN WHY WE'RE GOING TO THE LAB ON A GORGEOUS DAY LIKE THIS?

I TOLD YOU, CLAVE. THE LAB IS A MESS, AND RAINY DAYS ARE GREAT FOR *SPRING CLEANING!*

IT'S NOT *RAINING!* IT'S NOT EVEN CLOUDY!

JUST WAIT... 3,

2,

1.

RRRummbbble......

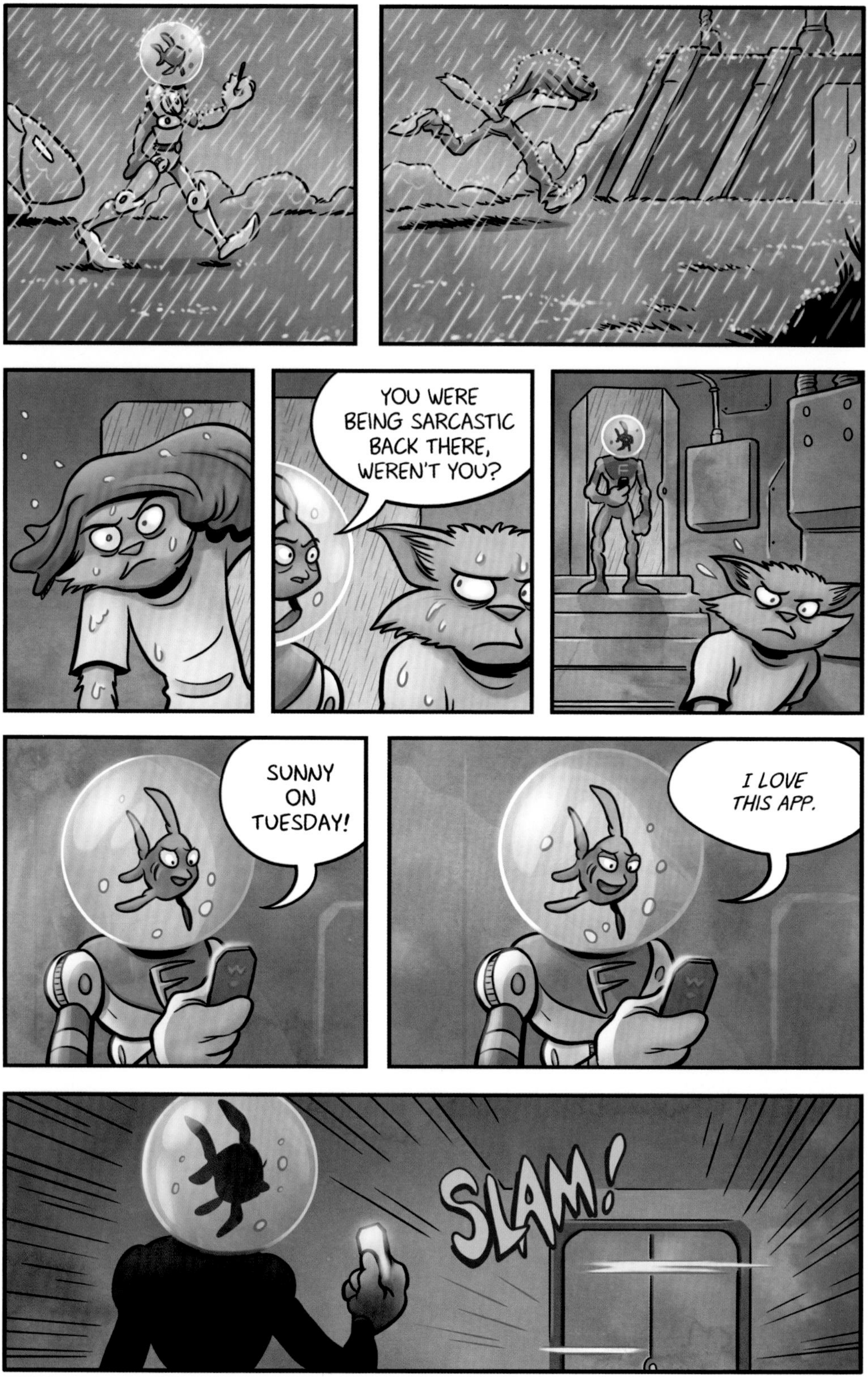
YOU WERE BEING SARCASTIC BACK THERE, WEREN'T YOU?
SUNNY ON TUESDAY!
I LOVE THIS APP.
SLAM!

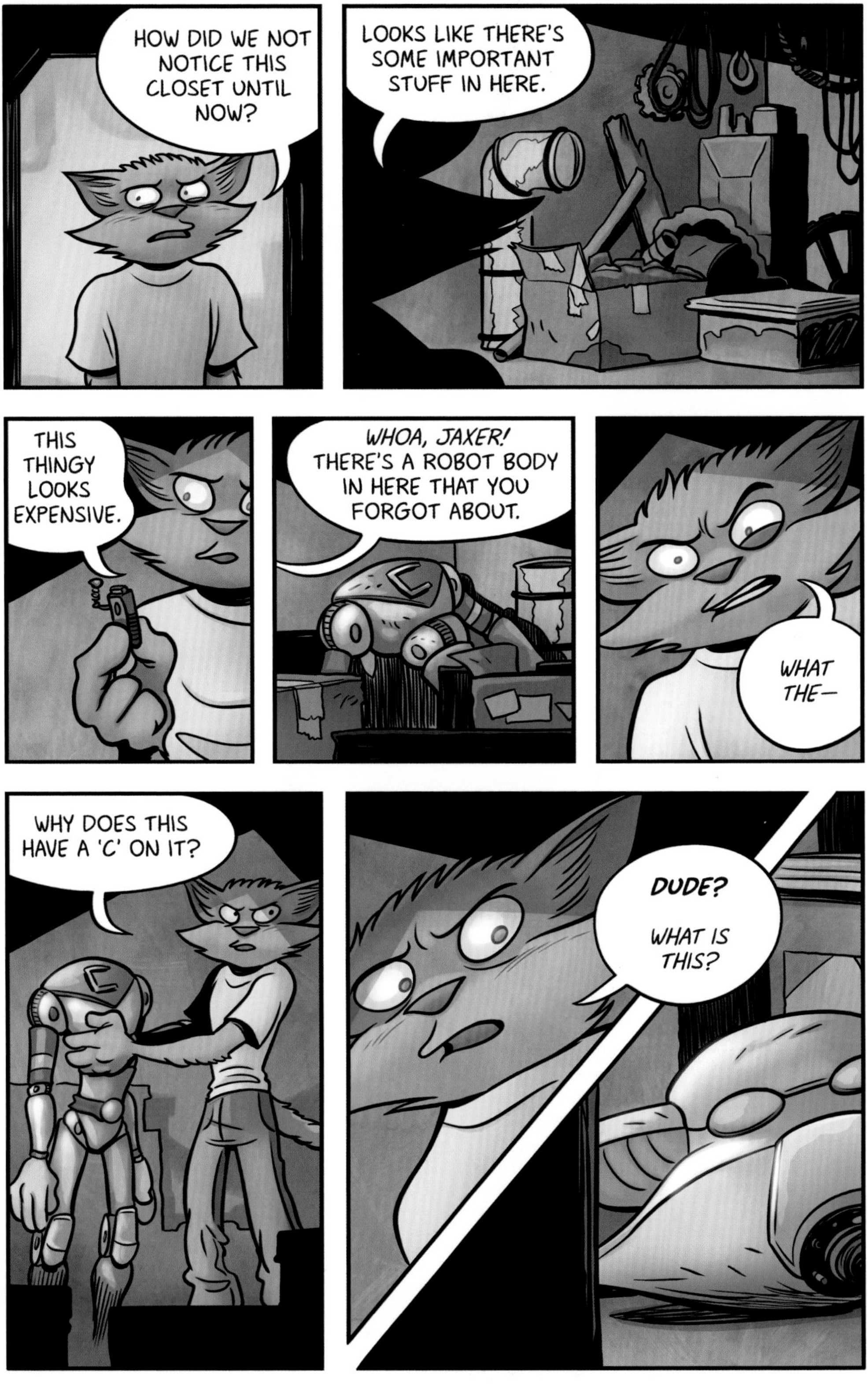
HOW DID WE NOT NOTICE THIS CLOSET UNTIL NOW?
LOOKS LIKE THERE'S SOME IMPORTANT STUFF IN HERE.
THIS THINGY LOOKS EXPENSIVE.
WHOA, JAXER! THERE'S A ROBOT BODY IN HERE THAT YOU FORGOT ABOUT.
WHAT THE—
WHY DOES THIS HAVE A 'C' ON IT?
DUDE?
WHAT IS THIS?

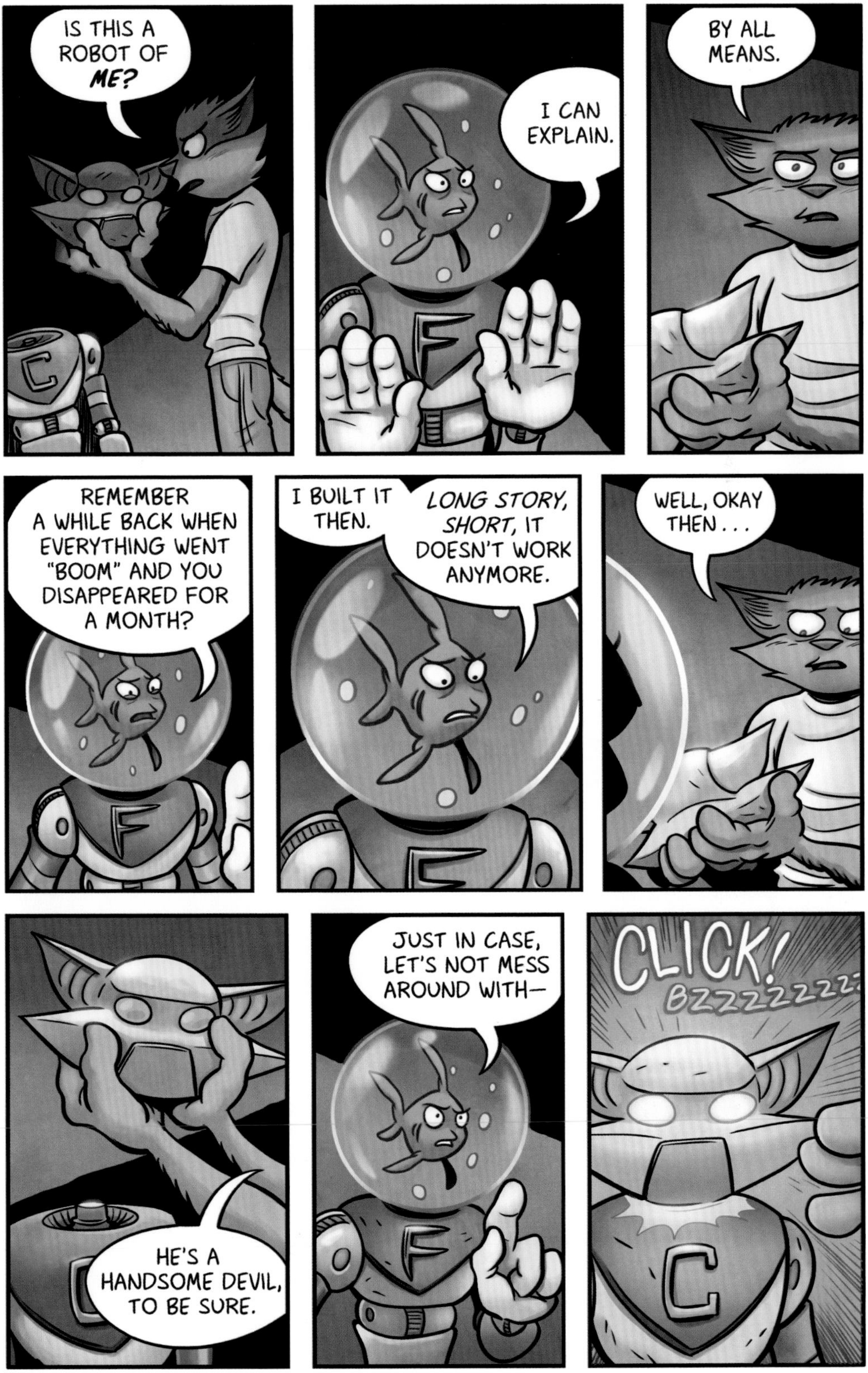

IS THIS A ROBOT OF ME?
I CAN EXPLAIN.
BY ALL MEANS.
REMEMBER A WHILE BACK WHEN EVERYTHING WENT "BOOM" AND YOU DISAPPEARED FOR A MONTH?
I BUILT IT THEN.
LONG STORY, SHORT, IT DOESN'T WORK ANYMORE.
WELL, OKAY THEN . . .
HE'S A HANDSOME DEVIL, TO BE SURE.
JUST IN CASE, LET'S NOT MESS AROUND WITH—
CLICK!
BZZZZZZZ

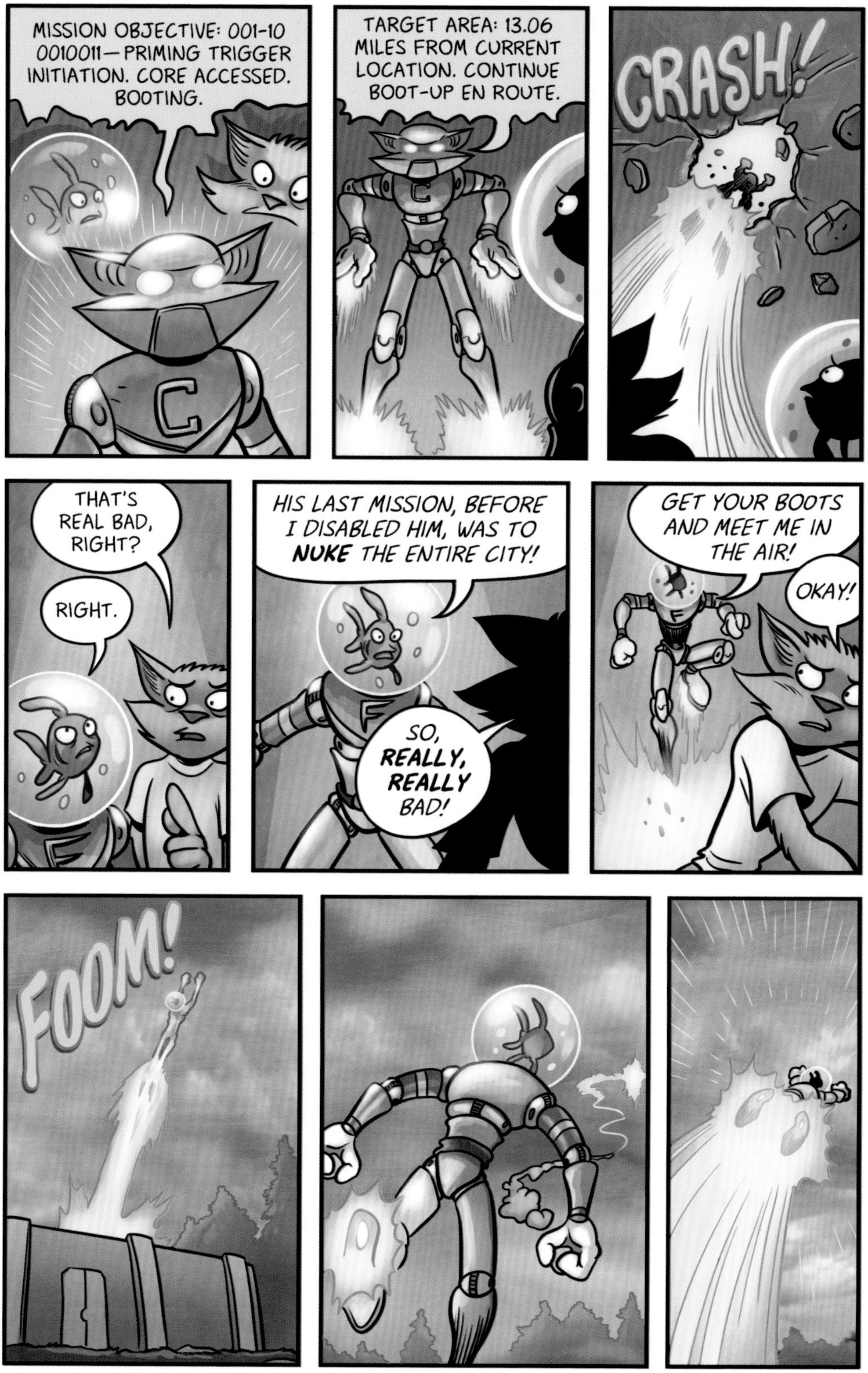
MISSION OBJECTIVE: 001-10 0010011—PRIMING TRIGGER INITIATION. CORE ACCESSED. BOOTING.
TARGET AREA: 13.06 MILES FROM CURRENT LOCATION. CONTINUE BOOT-UP EN ROUTE.
CRASH!
THAT'S REAL BAD, RIGHT?
RIGHT.
HIS LAST MISSION, BEFORE I DISABLED HIM, WAS TO NUKE THE ENTIRE CITY!
SO, REALLY, REALLY BAD!
GET YOUR BOOTS AND MEET ME IN THE AIR!
OKAY!
FOOM!

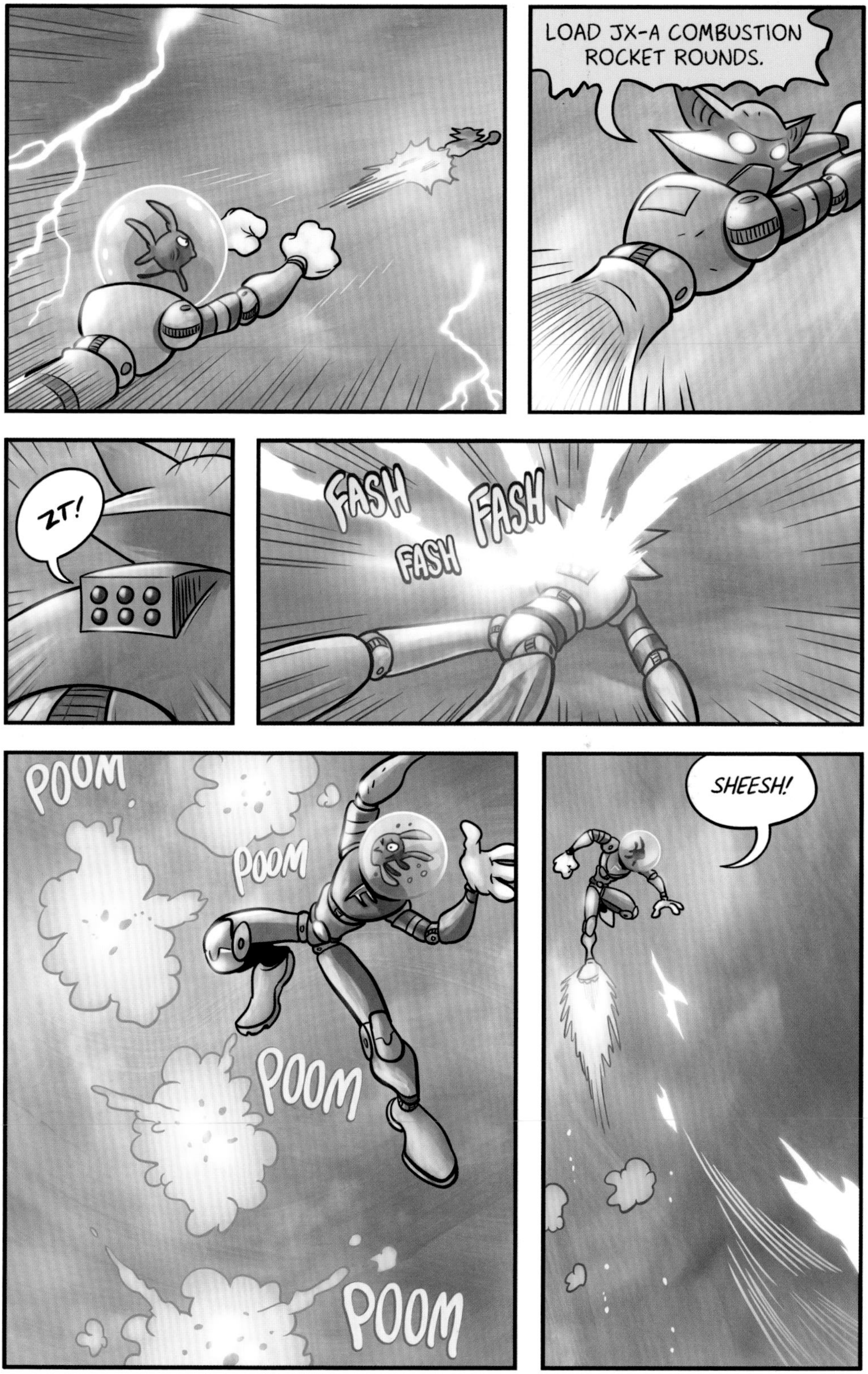

LOAD JX-A COMBUSTION ROCKET ROUNDS.
ZT!
FASH
FASH
FASH
POOM
POOM
POOM
POOM
SHEESH!

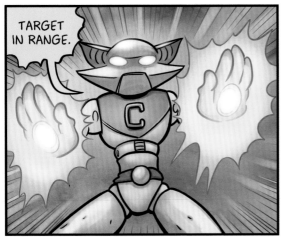

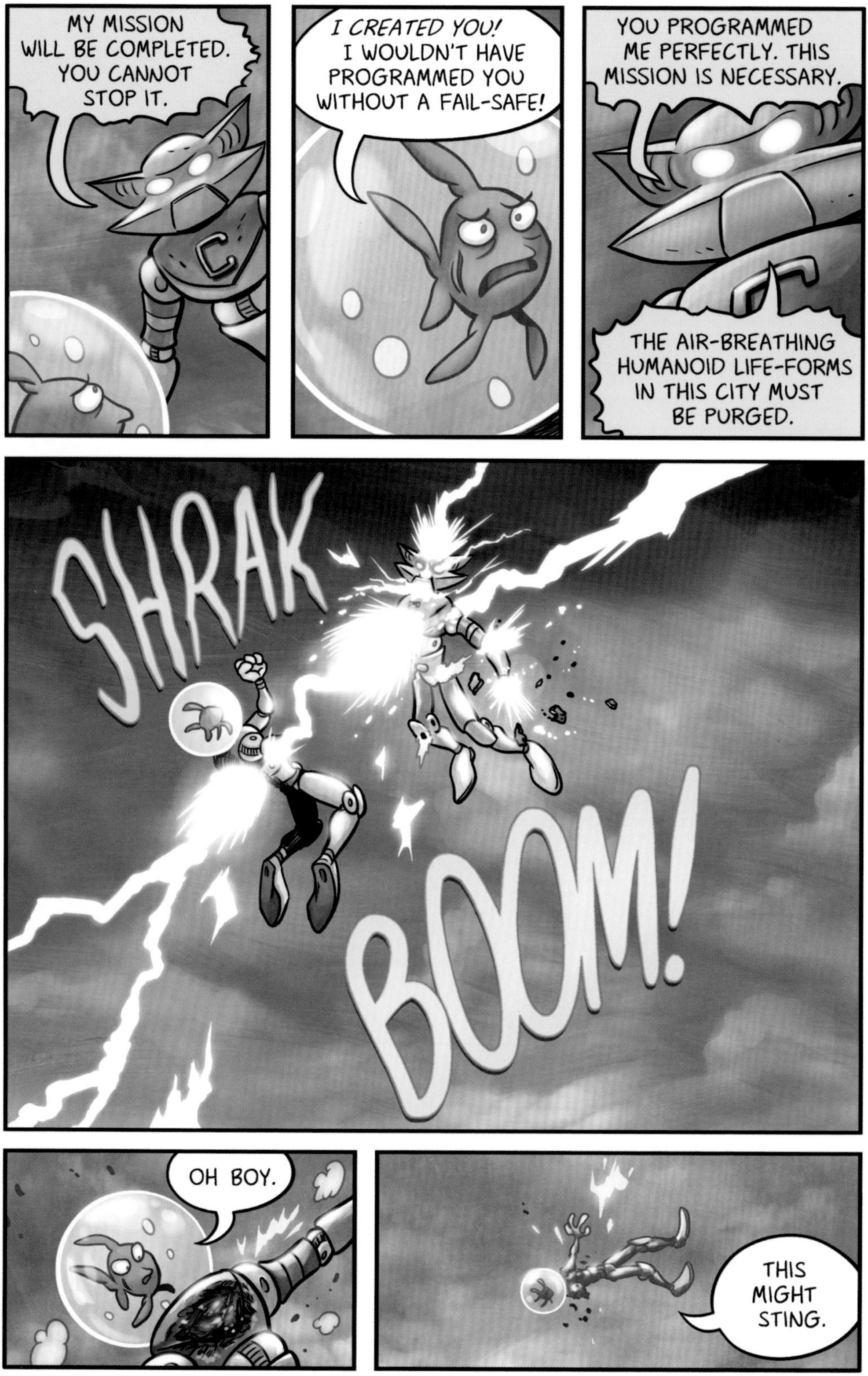
MY MISSION WILL BE COMPLETED. YOU CANNOT STOP IT.
I CREATED YOU! I WOULDN'T HAVE PROGRAMMED YOU WITHOUT A FAIL-SAFE!
YOU PROGRAMMED ME PERFECTLY. THIS MISSION IS NECESSARY.
THE AIR-BREATHING HUMANOID LIFE-FORMS IN THIS CITY MUST BE PURGED.
SHRAK
BOOM!
OH BOY.
THIS MIGHT STING.

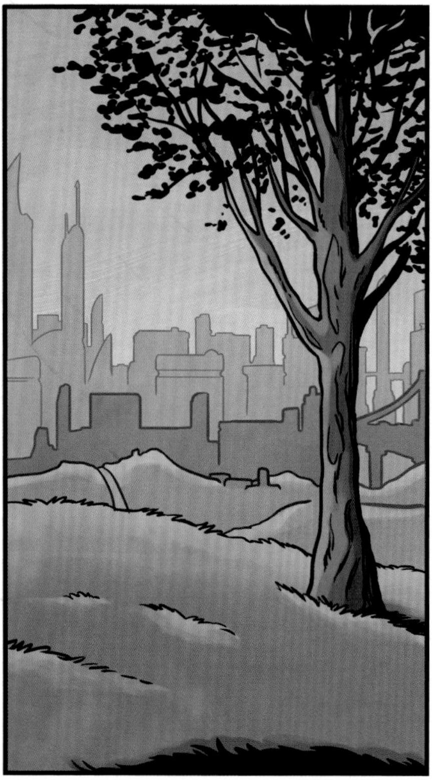

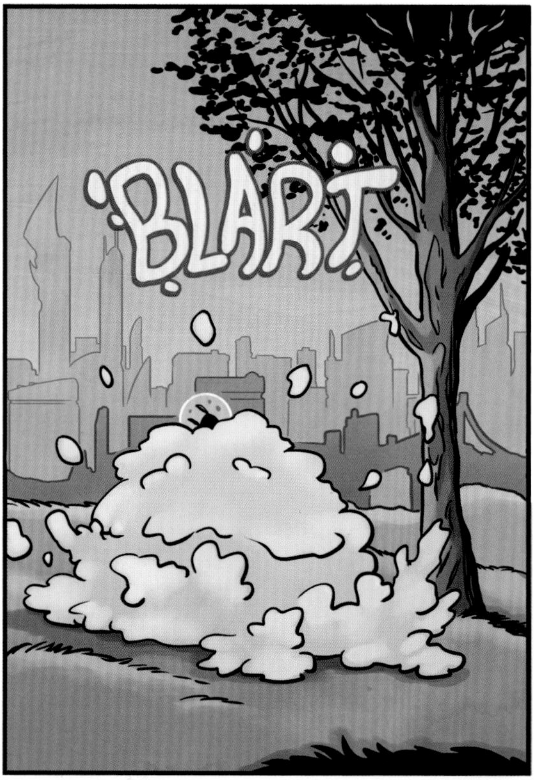
BLART

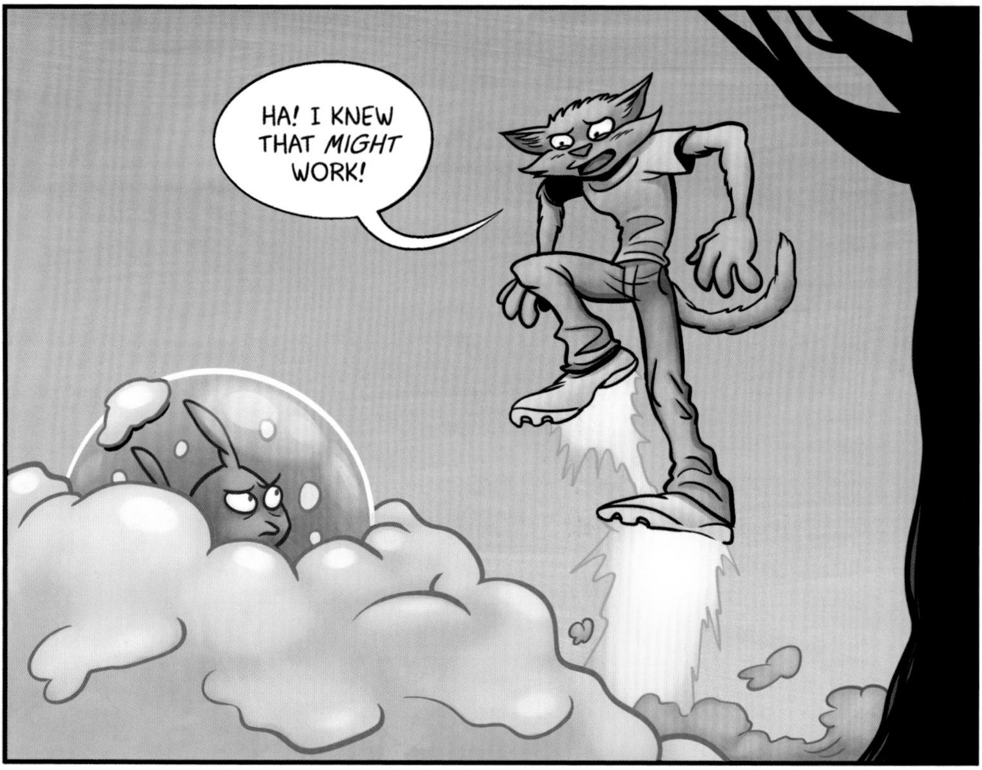
HA! I KNEW THAT *MIGHT* WORK!

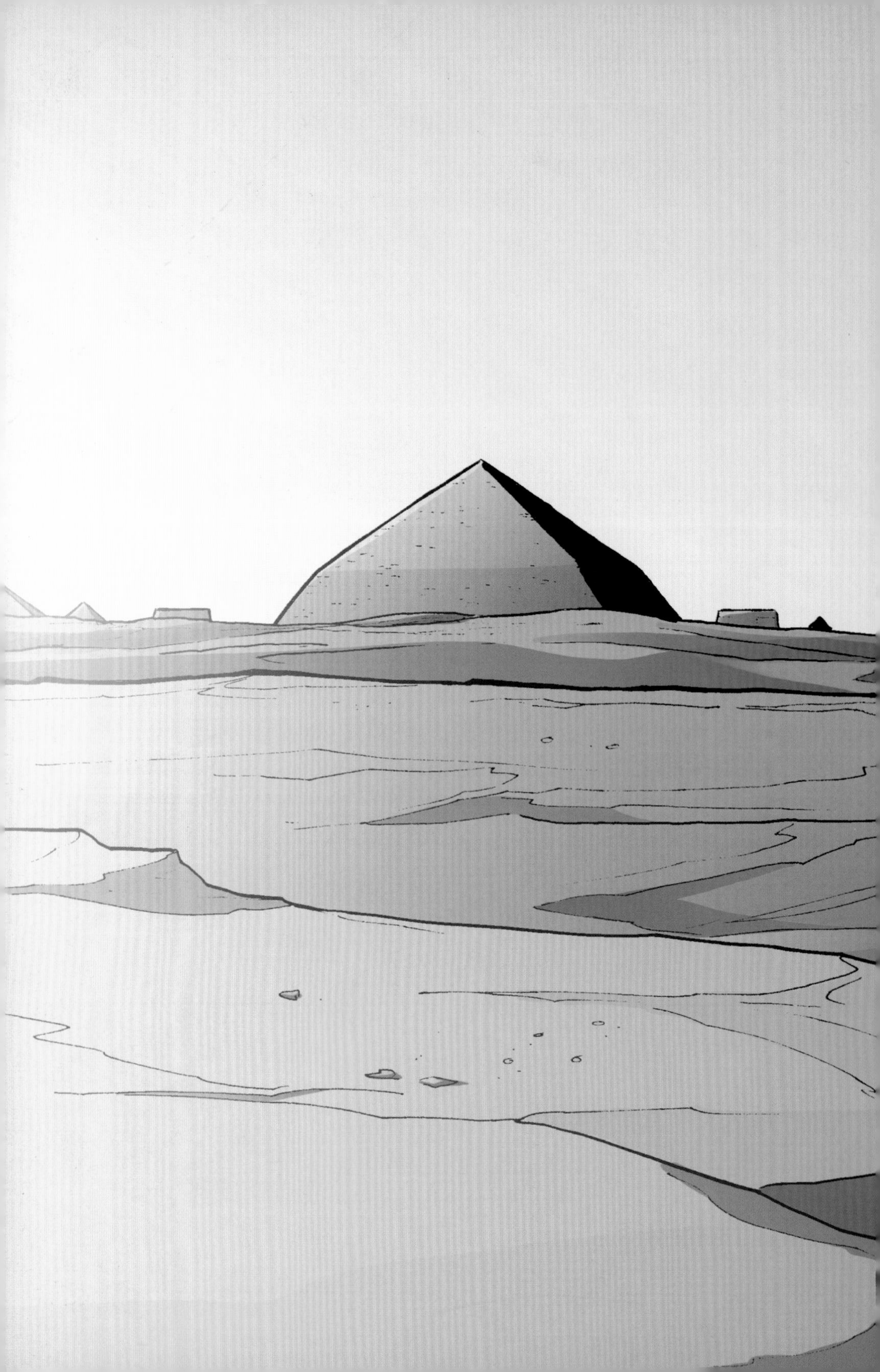

MASTABA

BY JOHANE MATTE

COLORS BY MARY CAGLE

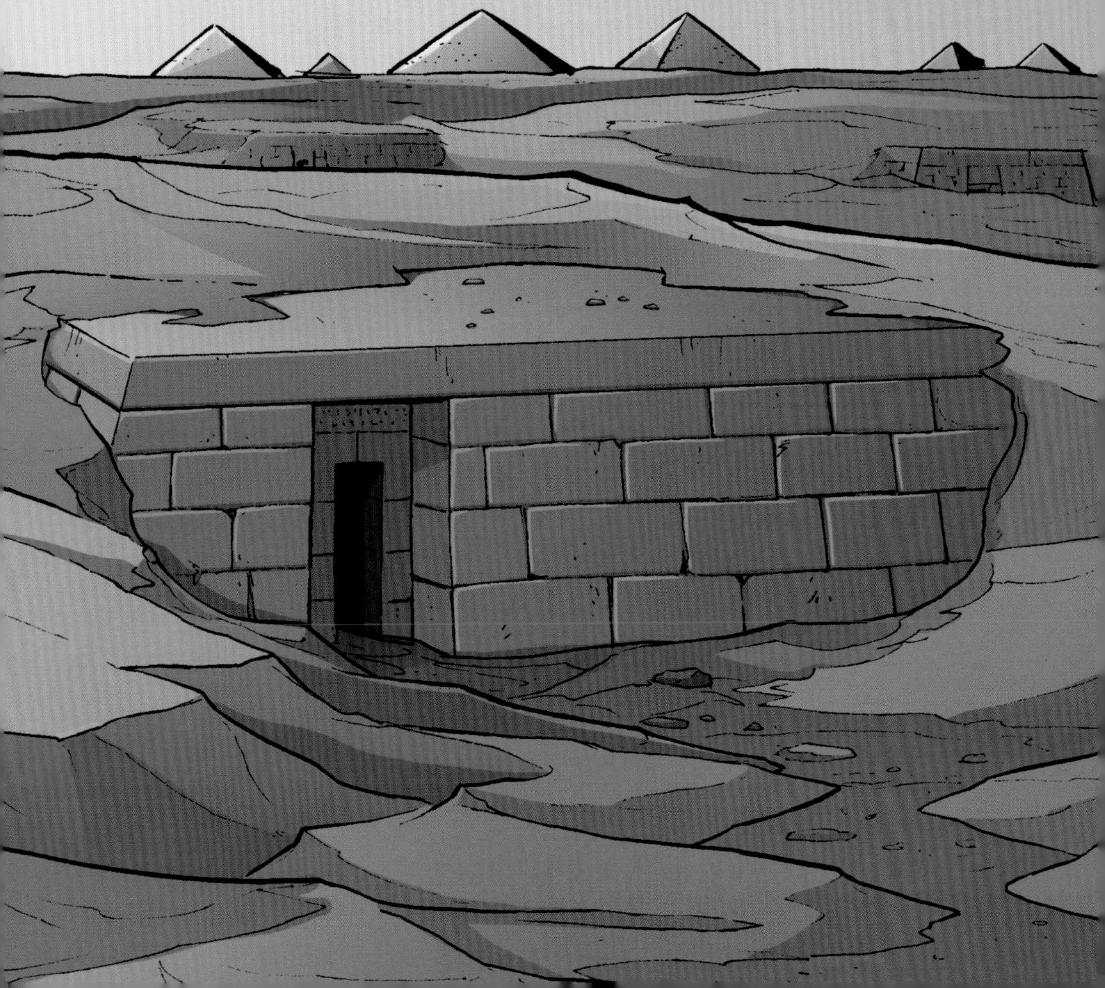

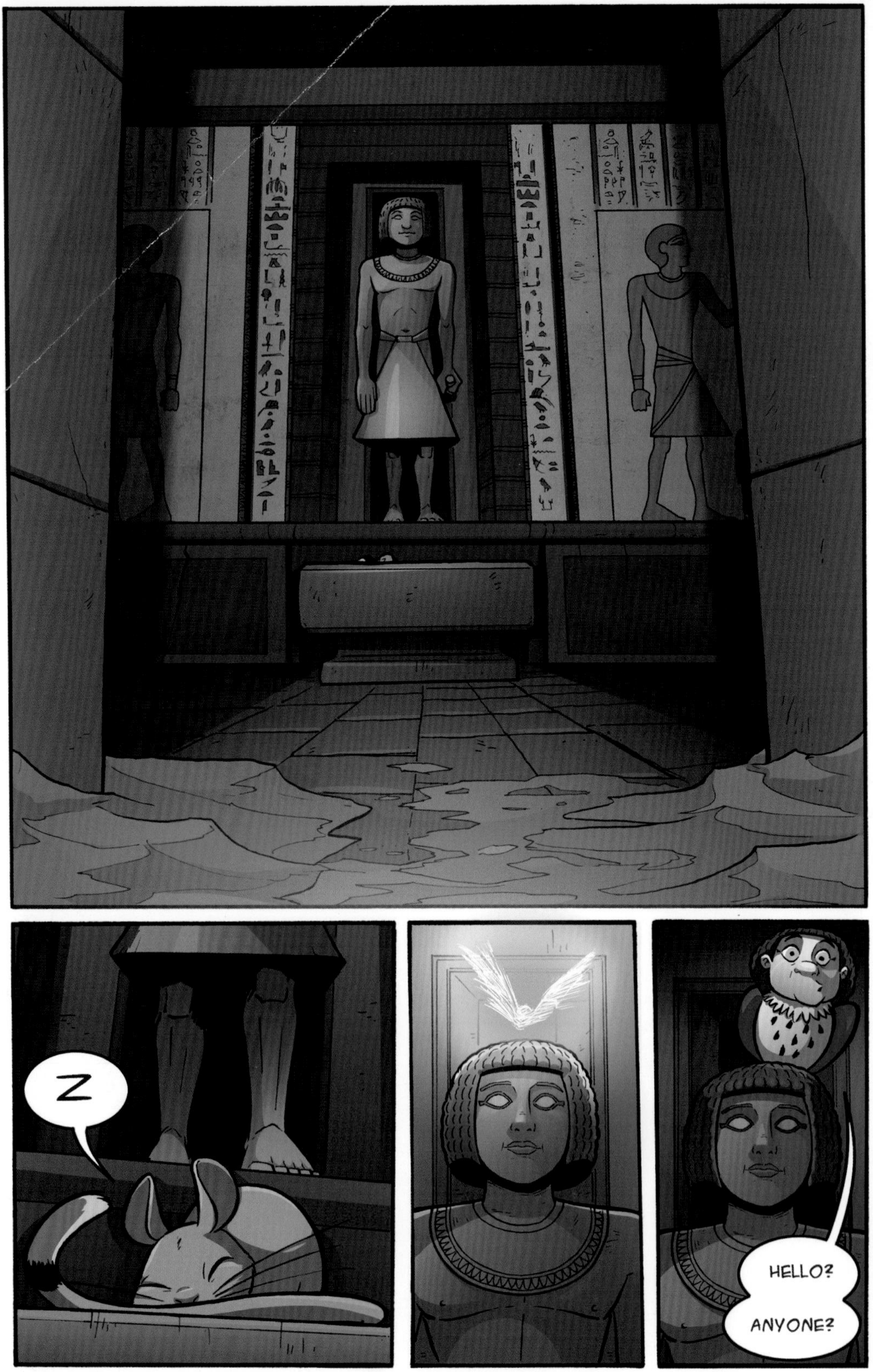
Z
HELLO?
ANYONE?

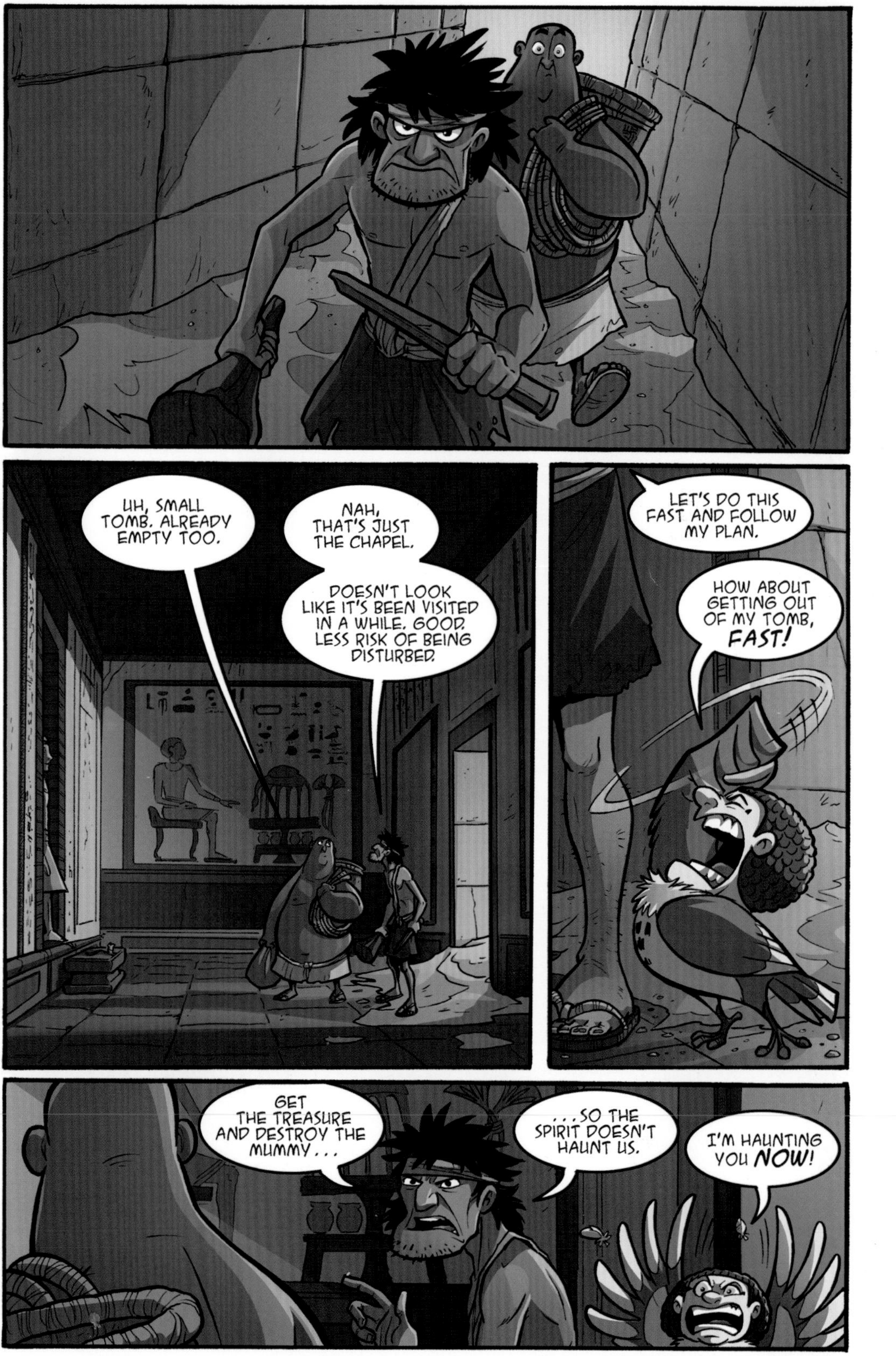
UH, SMALL TOMB. ALREADY EMPTY TOO.
NAH, THAT'S JUST THE CHAPEL.
DOESN'T LOOK LIKE IT'S BEEN VISITED IN A WHILE. GOOD. LESS RISK OF BEING DISTURBED.
LET'S DO THIS FAST AND FOLLOW MY PLAN.
HOW ABOUT GETTING OUT OF MY TOMB, *FAST!*
GET THE TREASURE AND DESTROY THE MUMMY . . .
. . . SO THE SPIRIT DOESN'T HAUNT US.
I'M HAUNTING YOU ***NOW!***

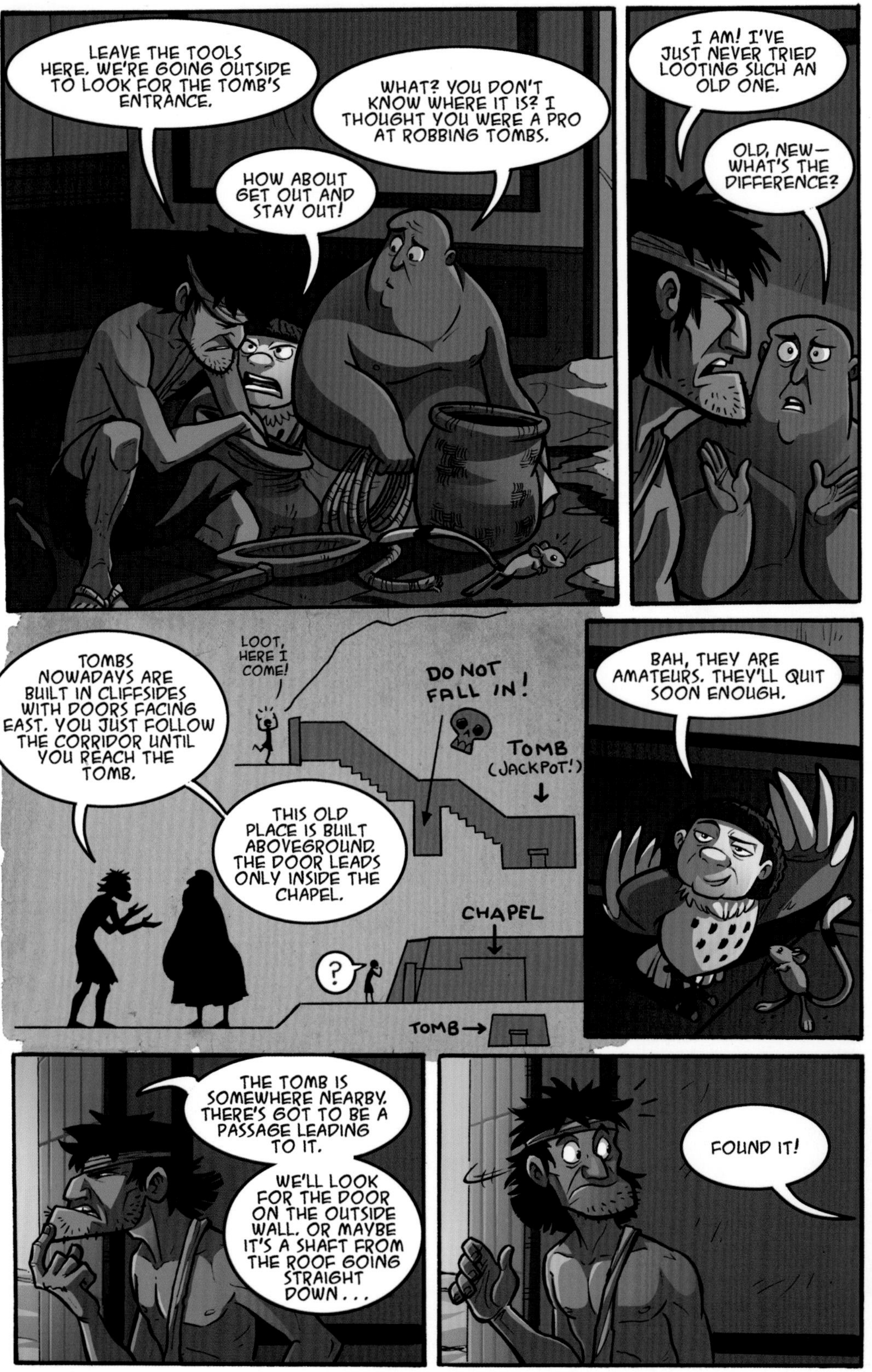
LEAVE THE TOOLS HERE. WE'RE GOING OUTSIDE TO LOOK FOR THE TOMB'S ENTRANCE.
HOW ABOUT GET OUT AND STAY OUT!
WHAT? YOU DON'T KNOW WHERE IT IS? I THOUGHT YOU WERE A PRO AT ROBBING TOMBS.
I AM! I'VE JUST NEVER TRIED LOOTING SUCH AN OLD ONE.
OLD, NEW—WHAT'S THE DIFFERENCE?
TOMBS NOWADAYS ARE BUILT IN CLIFFSIDES WITH DOORS FACING EAST. YOU JUST FOLLOW THE CORRIDOR UNTIL YOU REACH THE TOMB.
LOOT, HERE I COME!
DO NOT FALL IN!
TOMB (JACKPOT!)
THIS OLD PLACE IS BUILT ABOVEGROUND. THE DOOR LEADS ONLY INSIDE THE CHAPEL.
CHAPEL
?
TOMB
BAH, THEY ARE AMATEURS. THEY'LL QUIT SOON ENOUGH.
THE TOMB IS SOMEWHERE NEARBY. THERE'S GOT TO BE A PASSAGE LEADING TO IT.
WE'LL LOOK FOR THE DOOR ON THE OUTSIDE WALL. OR MAYBE IT'S A SHAFT FROM THE ROOF GOING STRAIGHT DOWN . . .
FOUND IT!

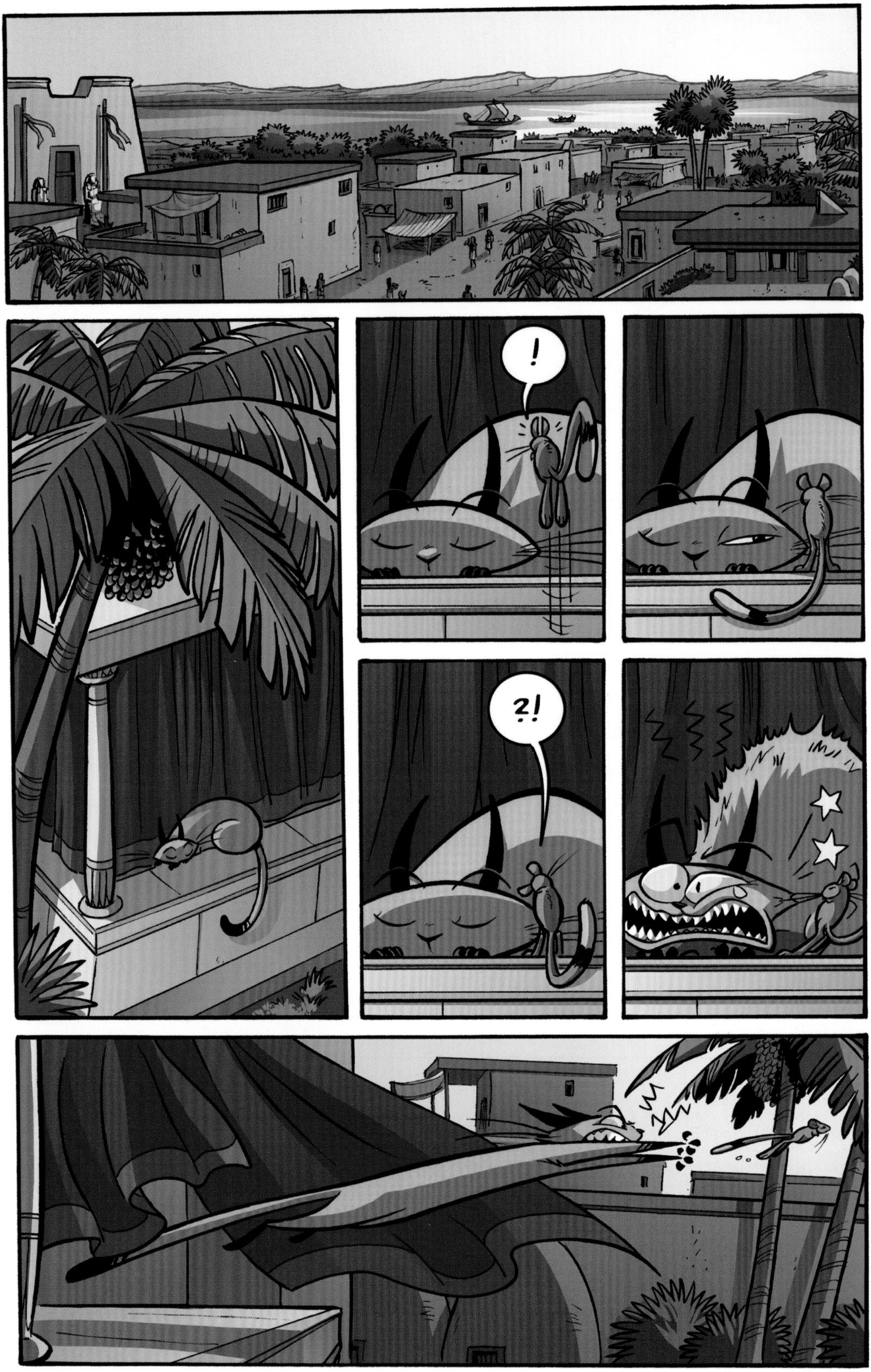
!
?!

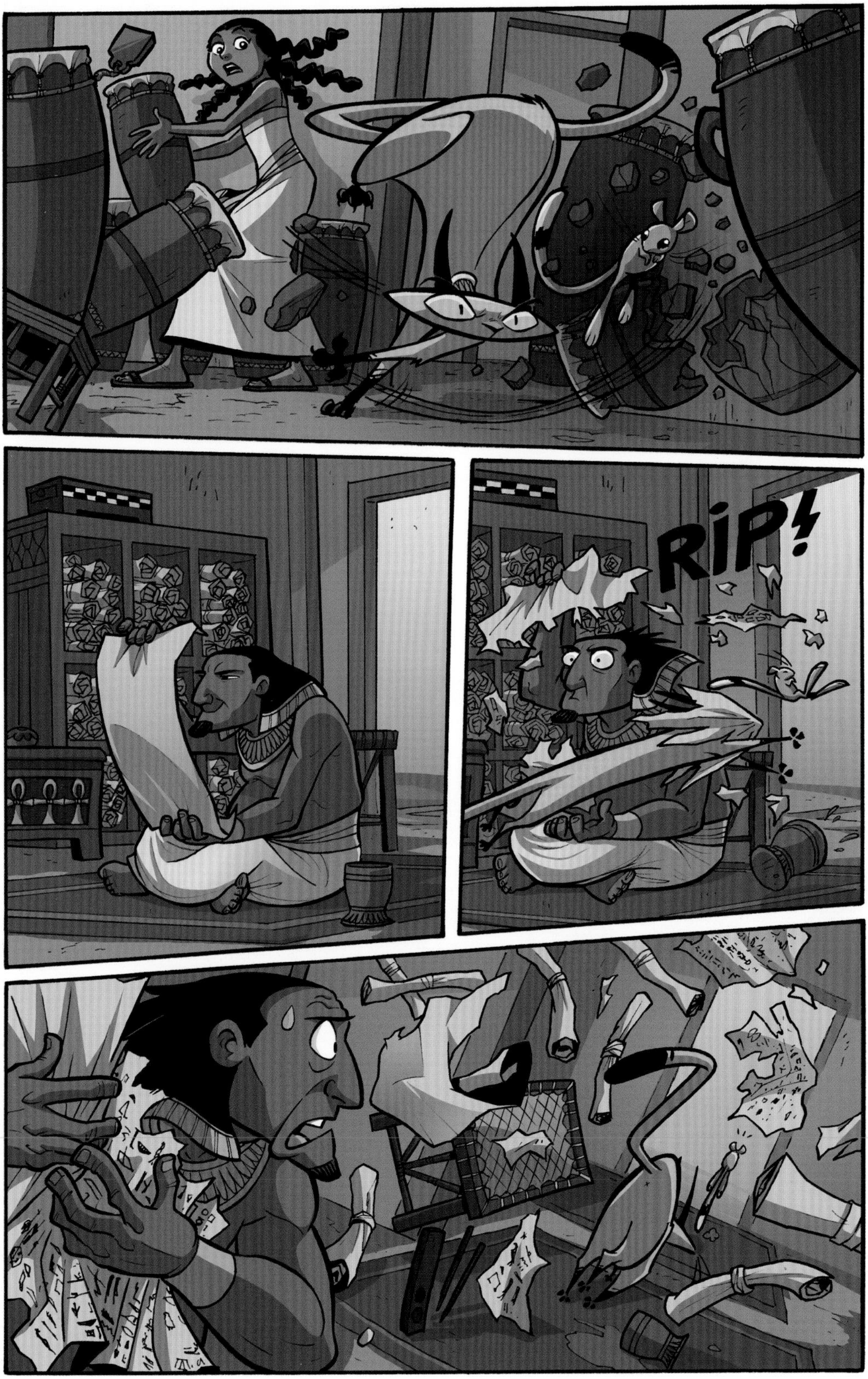
RIP!

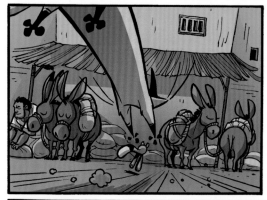

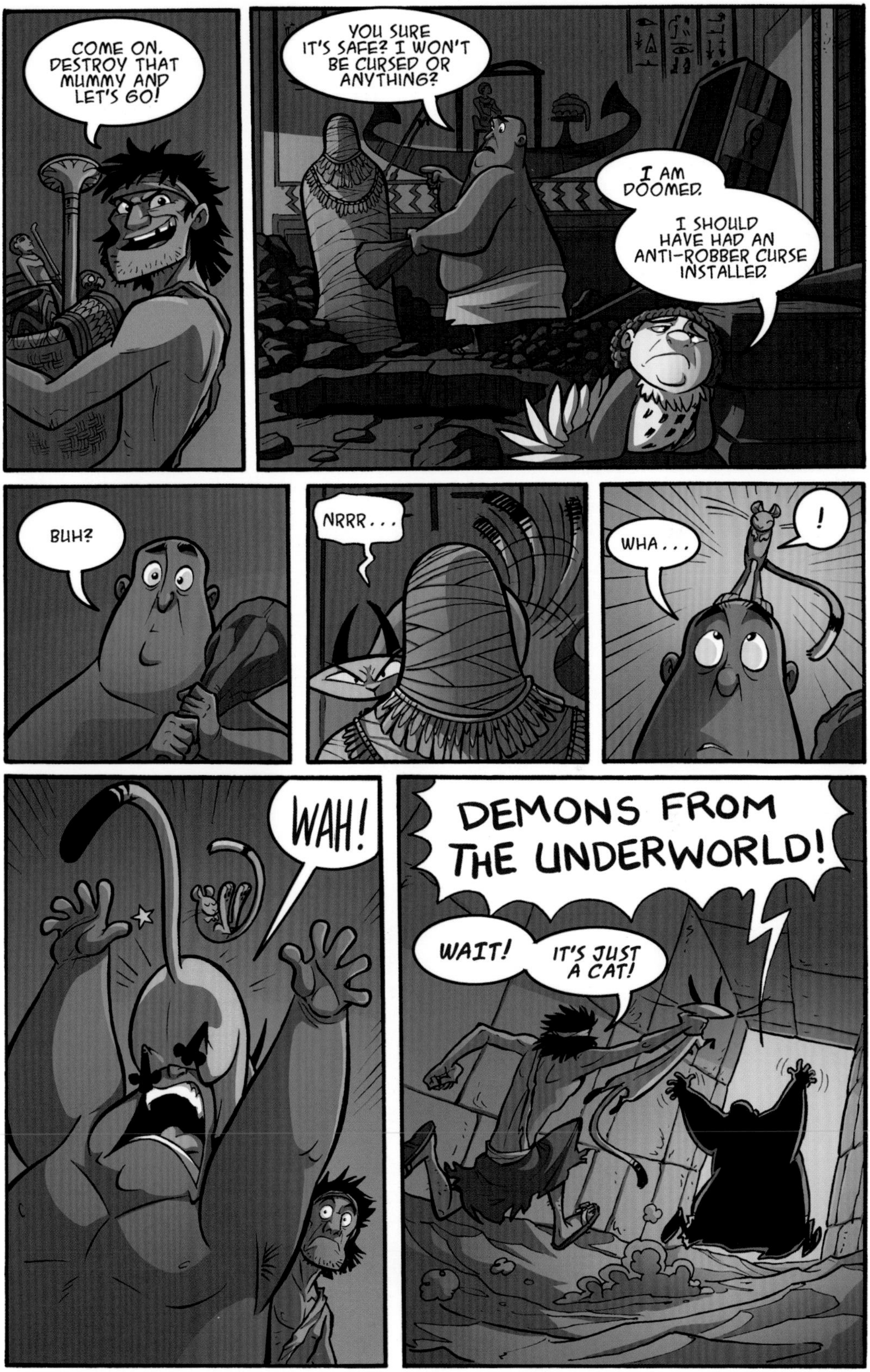
COME ON. DESTROY THAT MUMMY AND LET'S GO!
YOU SURE IT'S SAFE? I WON'T BE CURSED OR ANYTHING?
I AM DOOMED.
I SHOULD HAVE HAD AN ANTI-ROBBER CURSE INSTALLED.
BUH?
NRRR...
WHA...
!
WAH!
DEMONS FROM THE UNDERWORLD!
WAIT!
IT'S JUST A CAT!

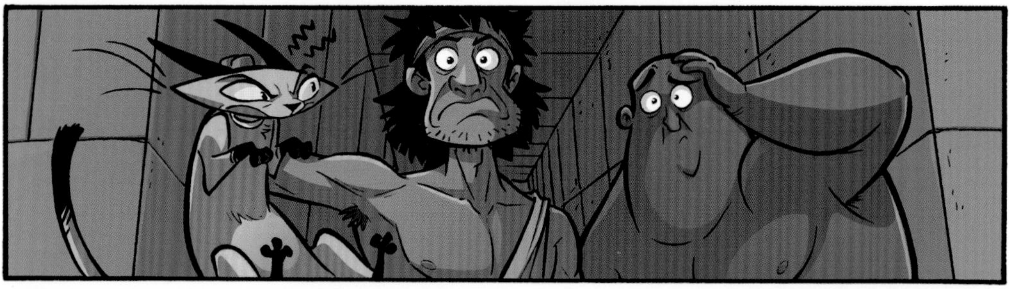

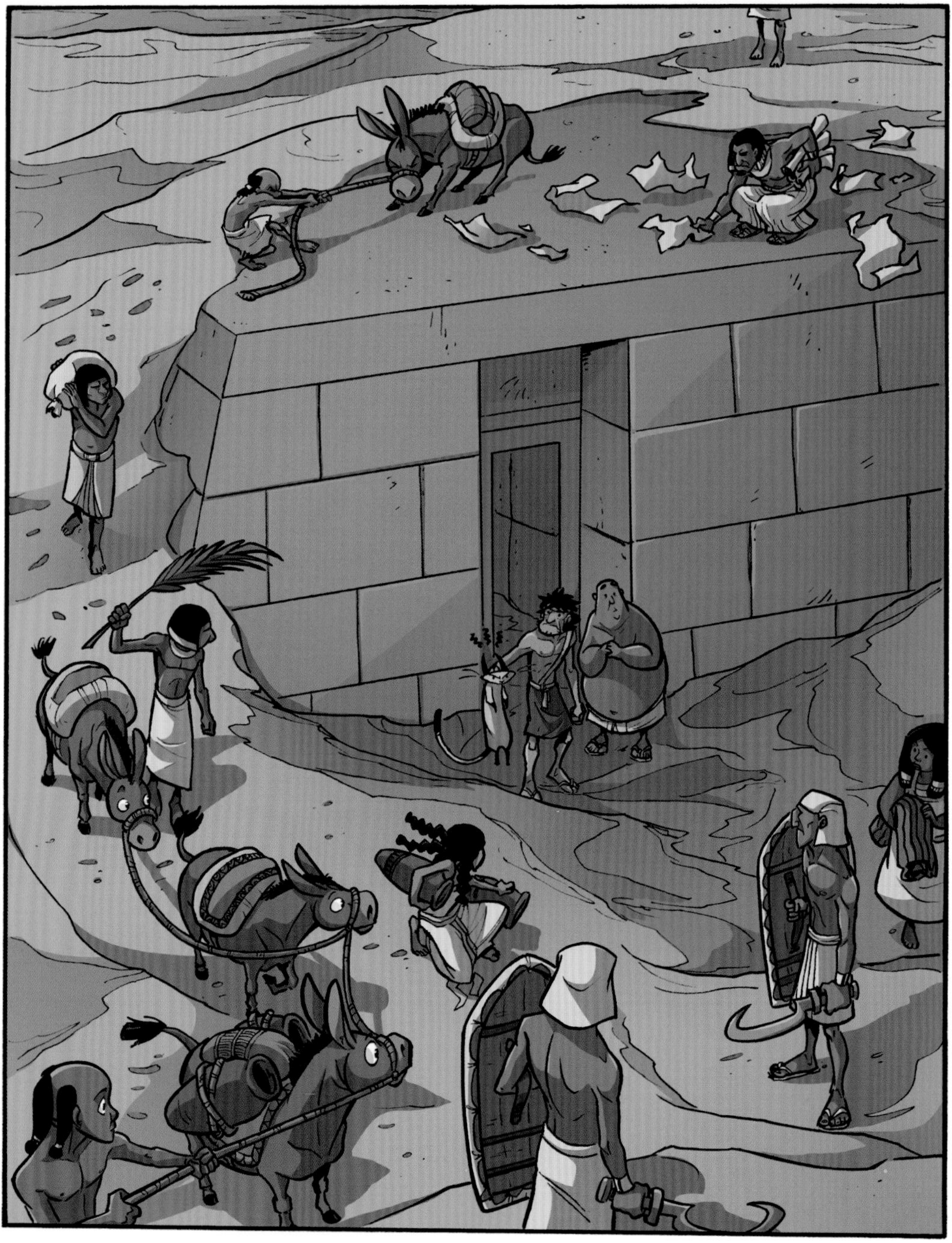

WHEN IS A DOOR NOT A DOOR?

BY JEN BREACH & DOUGLAS HOLGATE

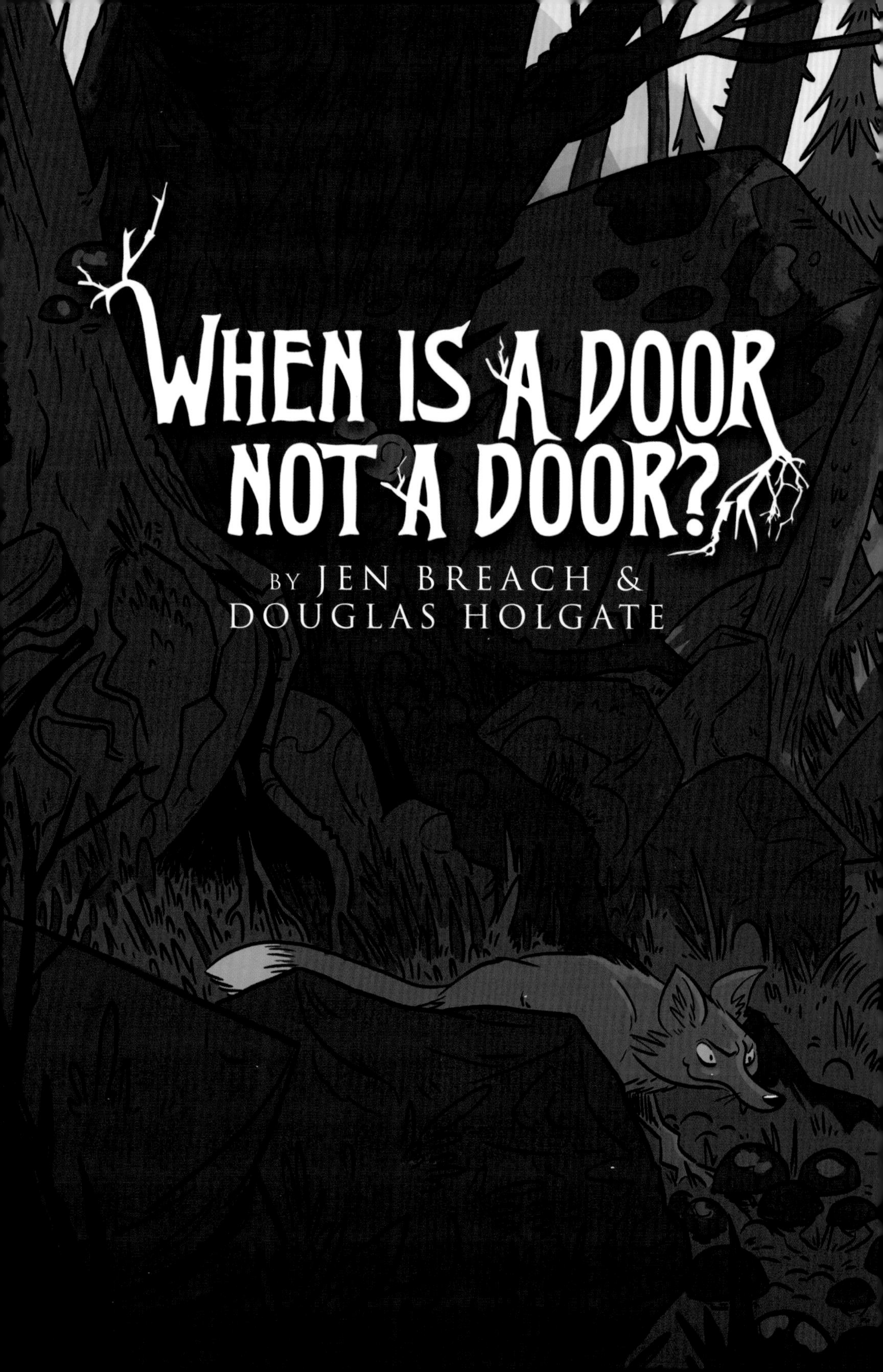

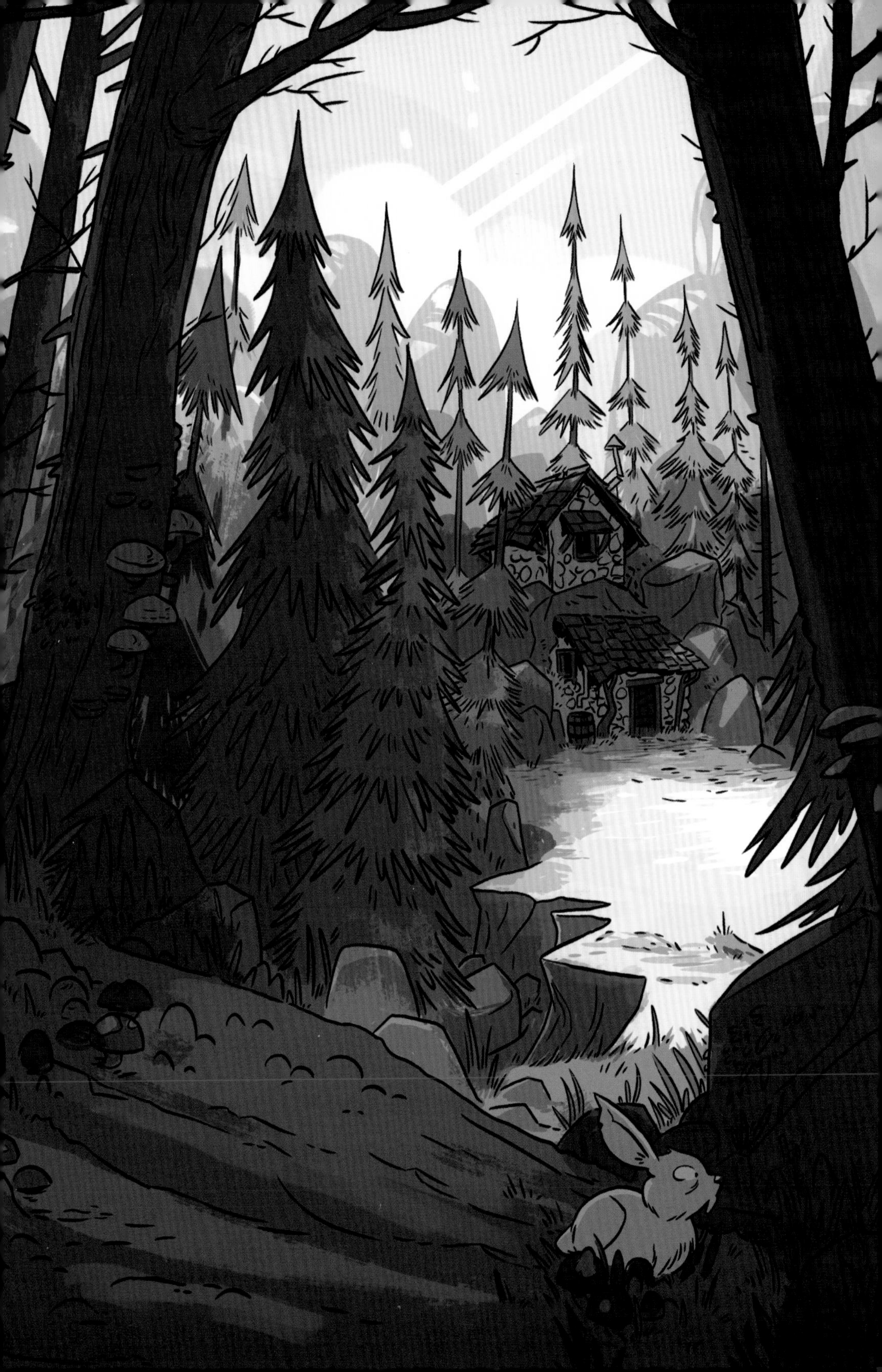

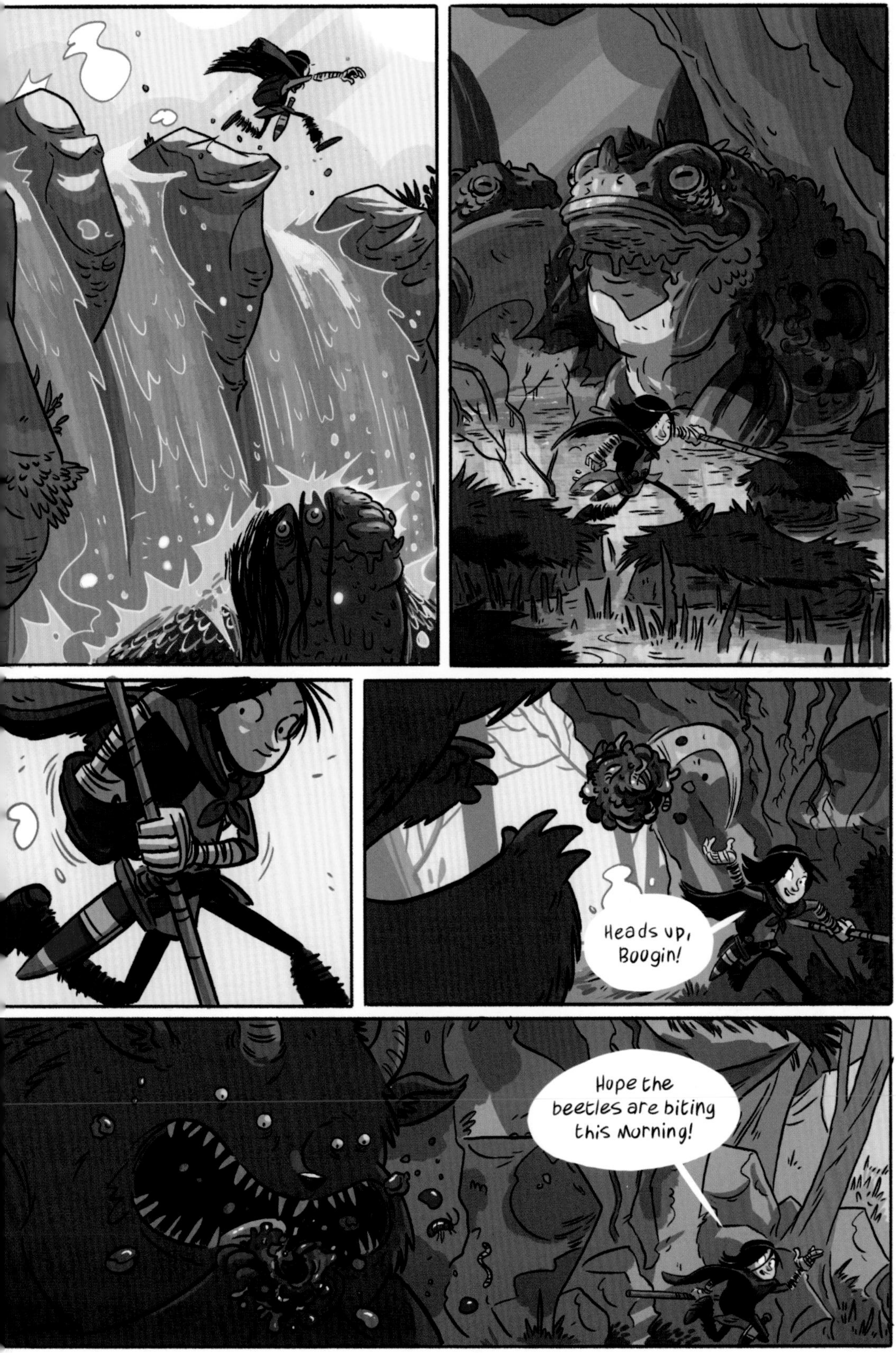
Heads up, Boogin!
Hope the beetles are biting this Morning!

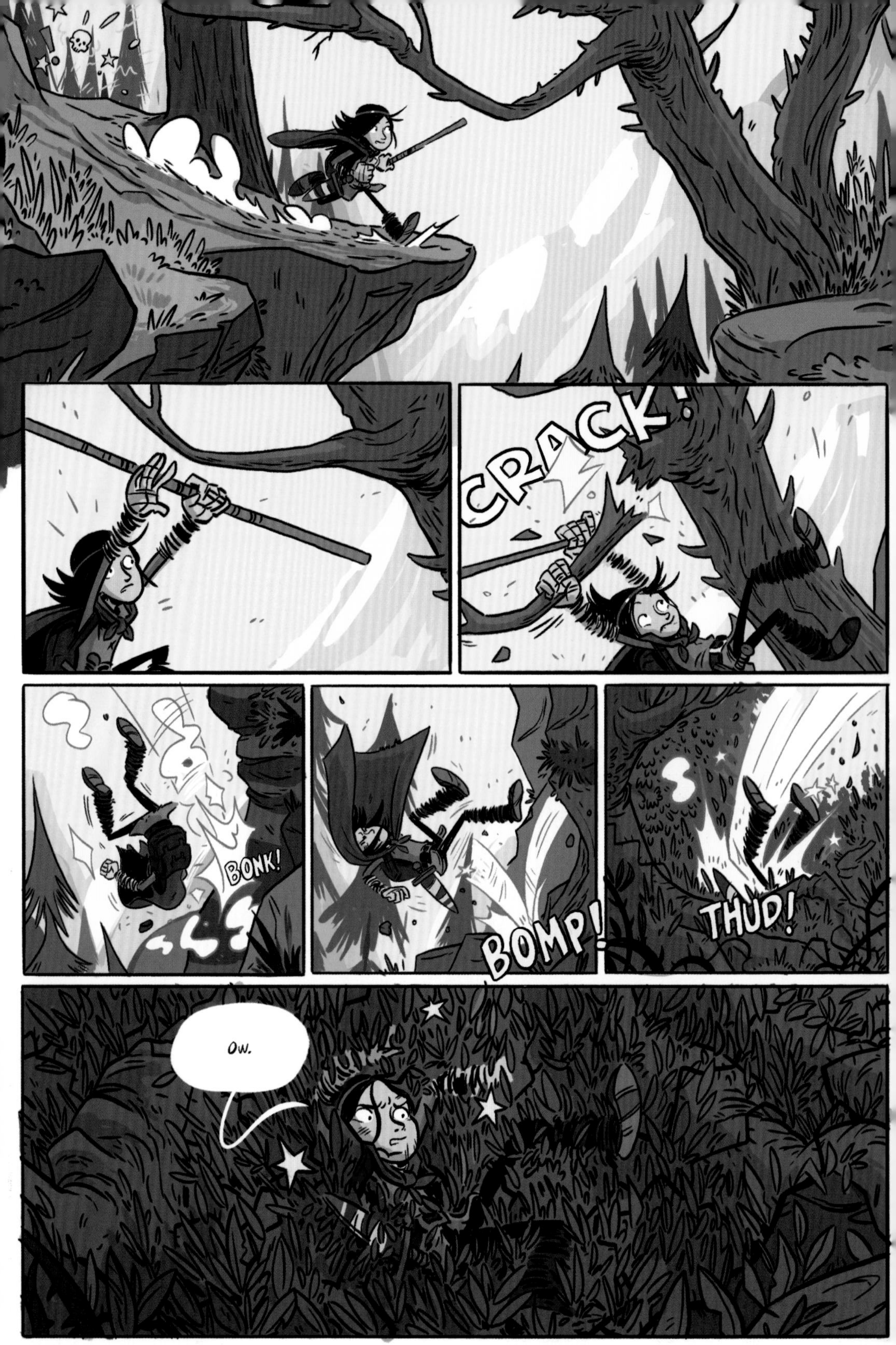

CRACK!
BONK!
BOMP!
THUD!
OW.

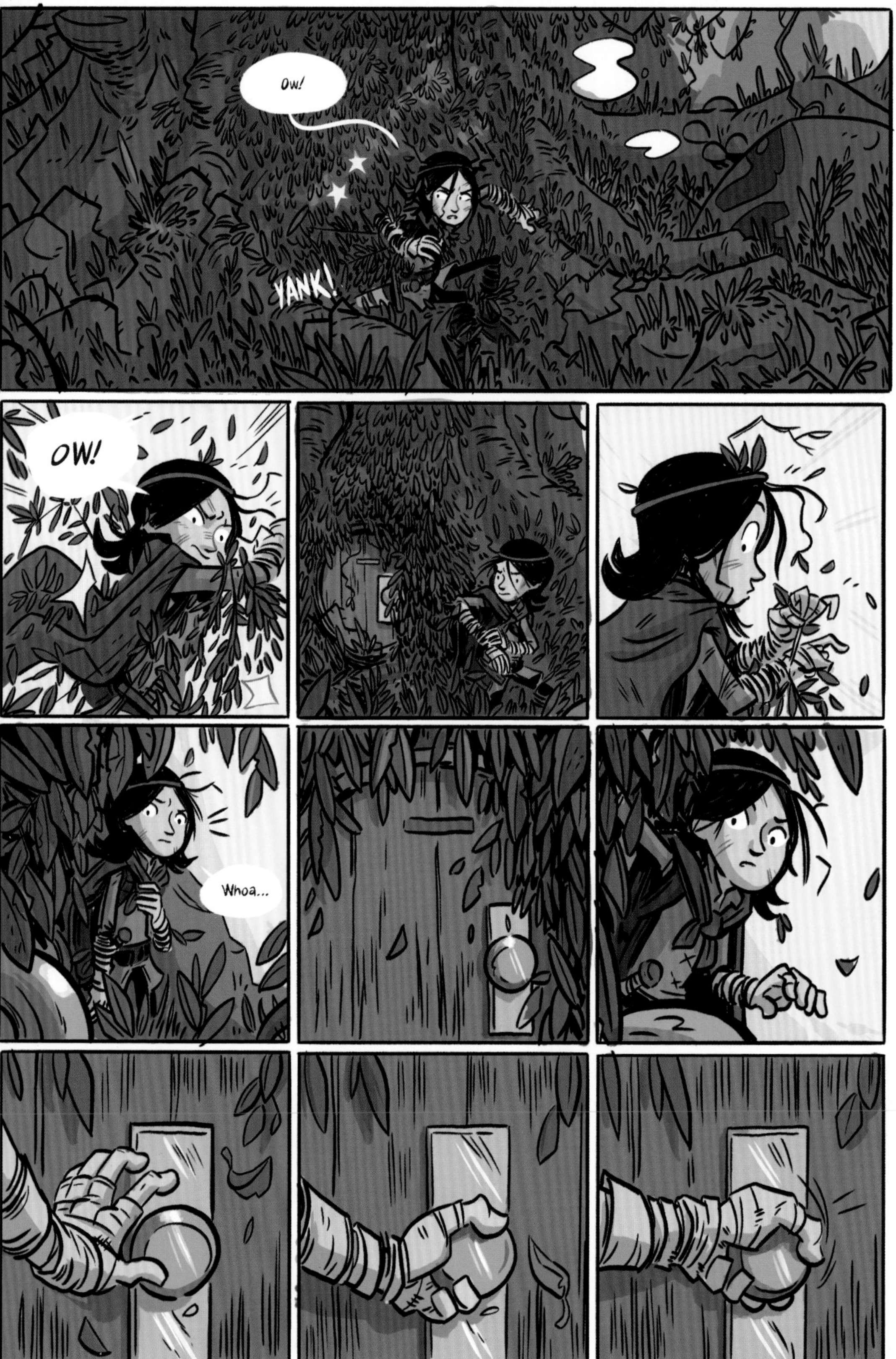
OW!
YANK!
OW!
Whoa...

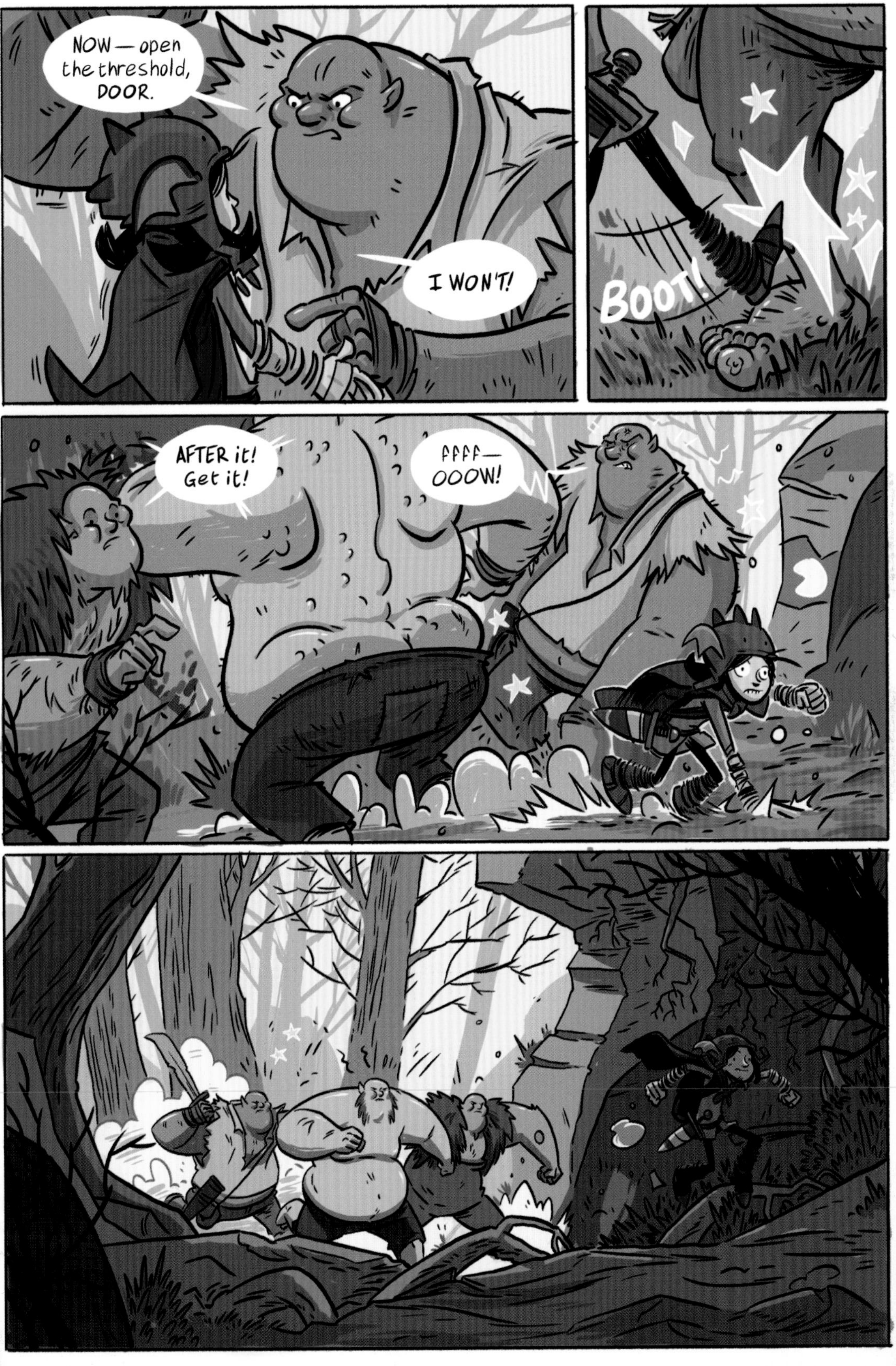
NOW — open the threshold, DOOR.
I WON'T!
BOOT!
AFTER it! Get it!
ffff— OOOW!

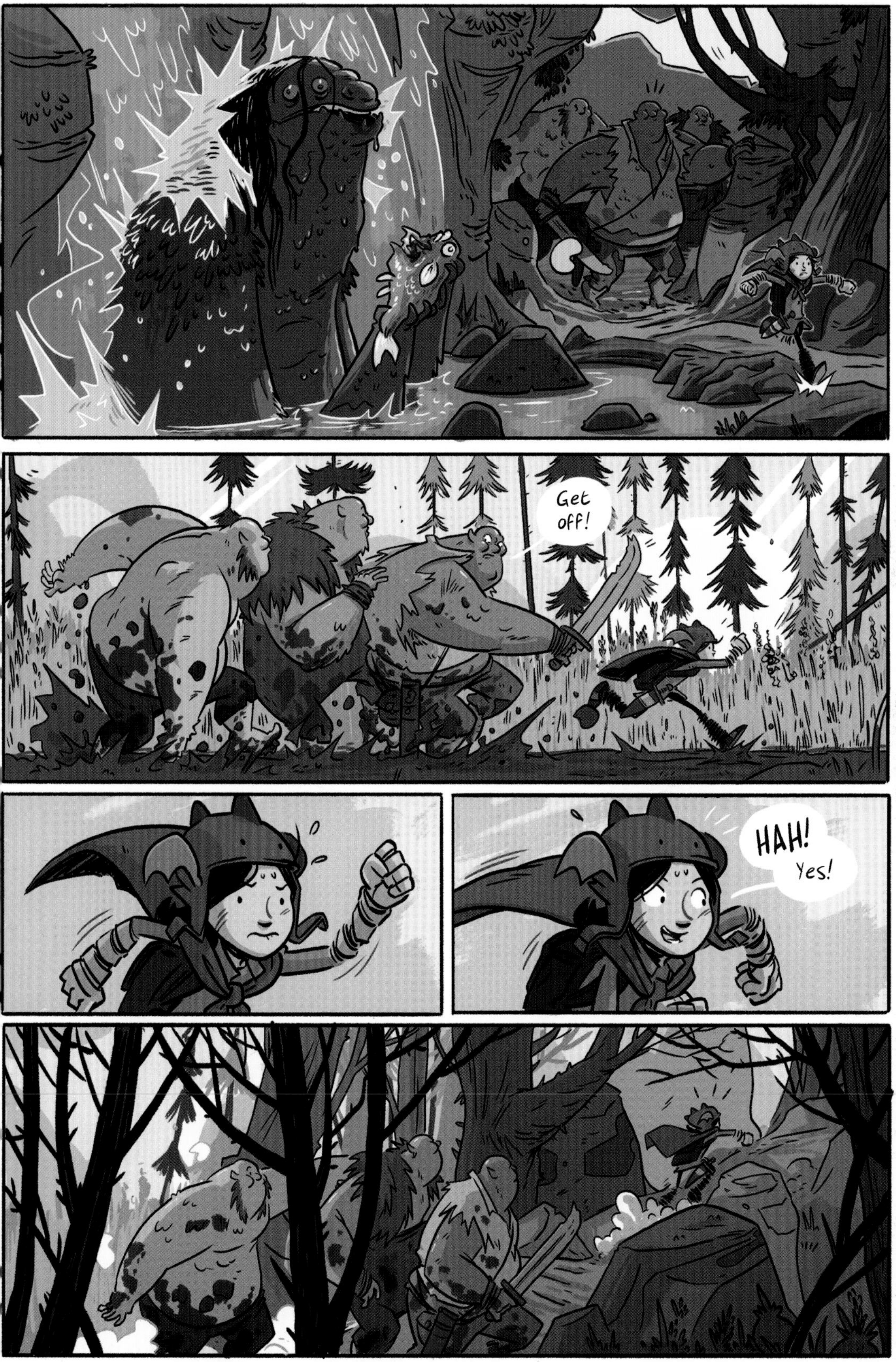
Get off!
HAH!
Yes!

ABOUT THE CREATORS

KAZU KIBUISHI is the creator of the *New York Times* bestselling graphic novel series *Amulet*. He was also the editor and art director of eight volumes of *Flight*, the groundbreaking Eisner-nominated graphic anthology. His comics collection *Copper* was a Junior Library Guild selection, and his debut graphic novel, *Daisy Kutter*, was named a YALSA Best Book for Young Adults. He recently created cover art for the new paperback editions of J.K. Rowling's *Harry Potter* series. Find out more about Kazu at boltcity.com.

JEN BREACH is a former archaeologist and librarian originally from Melbourne, Australia. Read more of her writing, including her comics project with Douglas Holgate, *Maralinga*, at jenbreach.com.

JASON CAFFOE, coeditor of the *Explorer* anthologies, is also a contributor to *Explorer: The Mystery Boxes*, *Explorer: The Lost Islands*, and the *Flight* anthologies. He is the lead production assistant for the *Amulet* series. Visit him at jcaffoe.tumblr.com.

STEVE HAMAKER is the Eisner- and Harvey Award–nominated colorist of the *Bone* graphic novel series by Jeff Smith. Other coloring work includes Coldplay's *Mylo Xyloto* comic series and *Table Titans* by Scott Kurtz. Links to more of his work can be found at steve-hamaker.com.

FAITH ERIN HICKS's previous works include *The War at Ellsmere*, *Friends with Boys*, *Nothing Can Possibly Go Wrong* (with Prudence Shen), and the Eisner-nominated *The Adventures of Superhero Girl*. She lives in Nova Scotia. To see more of her art, check out faitherinhicks.com.

DOUGLAS HOLGATE is the illustrator of many books and comics for kids, including *Case File: 13*, *Planet Tad*, *Cheesie Mack*, and *Zinc Alloy*. He lives in Australia. Find Douglas on your computer at www.skullduggery.com.au.

JOHANE MATTE is a storyboard artist at DreamWorks Animation. Her work appeared in *Explorer: The Mystery Boxes* and several volumes of *Flight*. Her credits as a storyboard artist include the movies *How to Train Your Dragon* and *Rise of the Guardians* and the TV series *Avatar: The Last Airbender*. Check out her art at rufftoon.tumblr.com.

JEN WANG is a writer and illustrator living in Los Angeles. She's the creator of the graphic novels *Koko Be Good* and *In Real Life*, co-written by Cory Doctorow. Explore more of Jen's work at jenwang.net.

* * *

MARY CAGLE colored "Mastaba." She is a comics artist and illustrator and a graduate of the Savannah College of Art and Design.

DENVER JACKSON helped color "Asteria Crane." He is a filmmaker, animator, and comics artist from Victoria, B.C.

NOREEN RANA colored "Two-Person Door." She is a Toronto-based freelance illustrator and user-interface designer.